P9-CCP-501

Lessons

by

Bonnie Geisert

Houghton Mifflin Company Boston 2005

Walter Lorraine Books

For Arthur and Noah

Walter Lorraine Books

www.houghtonmifflinbooks.com

Library of Congress Cataloging-in-Publication Data
Geisert, Bonnie.
Lessons / by Bonnie Geisert.
p. cm.
"Walter Lorraine books."
Summary: Following their infant son's sudden death, a farm couple is denied a Christian burial for him, and this secret continues to haunt the father after his second son is born.
ISBN 0-618-47899-X
[1. Baptism—Fiction. 2. Brothers and sisters—Fiction. 3. Farm life—Fiction.] I. Title.
PZ7.G2725Las 2005
[Fic]—dc22

2004015512

ISBN–13: 978-0-618-47899-6

Printed in the United States of America
QUM 10 9 8 7 6 5 4 3 2 1

Lessons

1

Something was bothering Dad. I noticed it after Matthew was born. Sometimes Dad looked right past me and he looked sad. Other times, he seemed deep in thought, his eyebrows furrowed, his eyelids blinking fast, like he was concentrating hard.

One day I asked Mom if Dad was mad at me or any of us kids. There were four of us older than three-week-old Matthew. Carol is almost fourteen. Kim is twelve. I'm Rachel, ten, and Susie is six.

Mom said, "No, no. Dad has something on his mind. Something serious and I can't talk about it right now."

I noticed that Dad seemed sad after he was around Matthew. The night before school started, I saw it again. After supper, while Dad was sitting in his stuffed leather rocking chair, Mom asked him to hold Matthew while she finished some things in the kitchen.

I was on the floor in my favorite spot between the couch and a lamp table with my back against the wall, reading a Nancy Drew book I had borrowed from Carol.

Susie had spread her new school supplies on the coffee table and was examining and reexamining them. Tomorrow would be the first day of school and Susie was starting first grade. She had been talking about her *very first day of school* practically nonstop for the last two weeks.

Carol and Kim were in their room, putting their hair in curls with bobby pins and making sure their clothes were ready. Carol was going to be a freshman in high school and Kim would be in seventh grade. I was going into fifth grade. Mom said my hair still looked nice from Sunday, so I didn't pin mine.

Dad wasn't very good at holding his new baby. He was afraid to move, so the baby stayed in the same position looking up at him. Matthew wriggled his arms and legs. Eventually he kicked his legs free of his plaid flannel blanket. All the time he fixed his eyes on Dad and made baby sounds in his throat.

Dad moved an arm and placed the blanket over Matthew's legs. "I think your mama wants your legs covered, little guy," Dad said.

Matthew's waving arms jerked at the sound of Dad's voice, then waved a little faster. Then he made more baby sounds.

"Are you going to be a boxer when you grow up? Those arms are pretty strong," Dad said.

Dad caught me watching him. "He throws a pretty good punch for a little baby," he said to me. Matthew wriggled his arms and legs faster.

Mom came into the living room with a baby bottle of milk in her hands. "Would you like to feed him his bottle?" she asked Dad.

"I'll let you do that," Dad said with a smile.

"It was nice visiting with you, little guy," Dad said when Mom took Matthew.

Mom settled in the small rocking chair without arms and laid Matthew on her knees facing her. She wrapped the blanket around his legs and body, leaving his arms free. She cradled his head in the crook of her arm and put the bottle to his mouth. He accepted it eagerly and made loud sucking noises. Soon the quiet rhythm of his sucking matched the gentle rocking of Mom's chair.

That's when I saw Dad looking at Matthew. Sadness came over him. He released a deep sigh and looked at Mom. She gave him a sympathetic smile. Dad shook his head slowly and returned to his *Newsweek* magazine.

Is something wrong with Matthew? I wondered.

Susie drew my attention away from Matthew. She had taken over the coffee table near Mom to check and recheck her new school supplies. She even had removed the newspaper that Mom had placed there, open to the page that announced the "Birth of a son, Matthew Lee, to Anton (Tony) and Leona Johnson," and had put it under the table.

Susie opened her box of eight primary crayons for the umpteenth time, touching the pointed tops.

"Susie, you're going to wear out that box before you ever get a chance to use your crayons," I warned.

She wrinkled her nose slightly but laid the box on top of her paper tablet with the Indian-head portrait on the red cover.

She stood the two unsharpened yellow pencils on their pink eraser ends as if to check that they were the same size.

"You don't need those pencils right away, Susie. Mrs. Bell has big fat red ones to use at the beginning of first grade," I told her.

She shrugged her shoulders.

"You won't get to use your tablet either, because you have to use school paper with wide spaces and dotted blue lines so you can learn to write the letters of the alphabet right."

"Raaacheeel!" Mom warned without raising her voice so she wouldn't bother Matthew.

I grimaced and went back to reading.

"Do *you* have everything ready for school tomorrow?" Mom asked me.

"I've been ready for a long time," I replied.

I couldn't wait for school to start. The fifth- and sixth-grade room was on the upper level of the school, next to the seventh- and eighth-grade room and the high school assembly hall with the glass doors you could look through.

And I was glad another hot, hard summer was over.

Still, there was a twinge, a knot of fear gnawing away in my stomach, as I wondered if I would slip easily into step with my friends after a summer of separation.

2

It was useless for Mom to try to get us to eat breakfast on the first day of school. We went through the motions, sat down at the table and said grace, but the four of us, with nervous stomachs and concerns about how we looked, were not in the mood for food. I spread some strawberry jam on a piece of toast and slowly nibbled it. Susie took dainty sips of her milk to avoid dripping on her new dress and to prevent a milk mustache.

Matthew started crying from his crib in Mom and Dad's bedroom at the far end of the hallway.

"Aren't you going to get Matthew?" Susie asked. "He's crying."

"A little crying won't hurt him," Mom answered. "It's good exercise for his lungs."

"I'd like to say goodbye to him on my *very* first day of school," Susie said in her very-important-manner voice.

"Oh, you *would?"* Mom teased. "Then I'll have to get him."

Dad was quiet this morning. He finished eating and was drinking coffee. He had that faraway look in his eyes. When Mom brought Matthew to the table, he brightened for a second and then looked sad again.

Susie smothered Matthew with a hug when Mom sat down. Then she kissed him on his plump cheek. "Are you going to miss me today?" she asked in that affected voice she had copied from adults when they talk to babies.

"You have no idea how *much* your baby brother is going to miss you, Susie," Mom said.

Matthew looked at Susie with wide-open eyes, and it looked like he tried to smile.

"I think you may have gotten his first smile, Susie," Mom said.

"It's quarter to eight," Carol announced. That was our cue to leave the table and finish getting ready. The bus would come at eight o'clock.

Matthew had Susie's finger in his grip and she was trying gently to get away. "Let go now, Matthew. I have to go to school. It's my *very* first day."

Really, it was her very first *half* day. Our first day of school is a half day.

We took quick turns in the bathroom brushing our teeth, and checked our hair and clothes in the mirror—Susie and I in our room at the end of the hall, and Carol and Kim in their room between ours and Mom and Dad's bedroom.

After brushing my teeth, I checked my hair and new dress in the bedroom mirror. I moved over when Susie came. The mirror reflected our sister images. We wore our new sister dresses—plaid with white collars, the hemline just below our knees. Susie's was blue and pink plaid, mine blue and green plaid. Our hair fell in smooth neck-length pageboys, both of us with straight bangs. I was a head taller, my hair was two shades darker, and my eyes were blue.

Susie smoothed her light brown bangs. Her dark brown eyes with long thick eyelashes quickly approved her reflection. She gathered her school supplies in her hands. "I'm going to wait for the bus in the kitchen," she said.

"Okay." I was glad to have the room to myself. That knot in my stomach tightened as I fiddled with a stubborn cowlick that made half of my bangs poke out in the wrong direction.

Despite my nervous stomach, I was glad that I would be in school instead of chasing cattle, making hay, pitching manure, fixing fence, and all the other jobs there were to do on a cattle farm.

"Here comes the bus!" Susie called from the kitchen, where she had been watching from the corner windows by Dad's place at the table.

That meant the bus was close to the mile turn and would be in our yard in a few minutes. I gave up on the cowlick, which had flattened a little. I picked up my school things and headed for the kitchen.

Susie was waiting by the door.

"No hug or kiss for your mother, Susie?" Mom asked.

"Oh, yeah," Susie said, as though remembering something she had forgotten. She gave Mom a hug, then kissed her cheek. Mom hugged her back with the arm that wasn't holding Matthew.

I could tell Mom was going to miss Susie. She hugged her like she didn't want to let go.

"How about me?" Dad asked.

Susie gave Dad a quick hug and kiss. "Bye, Dad," she said.

The rest of us were too old for goodbye hugs. "Bye!" we said and filed out the door, from youngest to oldest.

Blackie, our Border collie mutt, was there to greet us. None of us wanted to touch him, so he sat on his haunches by the door.

I felt sorry for him and walked over to pet him with my free hand. "I bet you'll miss us today too, Blackie."

"Yuck! Now you have germs on your hand!" Kim said, wrinkling her nose.

I reached out my palm and walked toward her,

aiming right at her new white blouse tucked neatly inside a new blue print skirt.

"Don't you dare!" she said.

I shifted my hand higher, threatening her blond hair with every curl in place around her face. "Don't you dare!" she repeated.

"Rachel, cut it out!" Carol said.

I let it go and lined up behind Susie.

It was a calm, warm morning, no wind to disturb anyone's hair.

The school bus was right on time. Eight o'clock, just like other years. The yellow bus with CRESBARD CONSOLIDATED SCHOOL on its side drove onto our cement driveway in front of the garage just a few steps from our breezeway door.

"Stay back until the bus stops," Carol warned an eager Susie. Carol acted and looked older than fourteen years. She wore lipstick, and her dark collar-length hair was parted on the side with a barrette holding it in place. Bangs fell obediently to the middle of her forehead. She wore a white blouse and a green print skirt with a wide belt around her waist. Carol looked like a high schooler.

We must have looked like an eight-legged caterpillar climbing into the bus after the door folded open. The four of us had black-and-white saddle shoes with white anklets.

"I see we have *four* Johnson girls this year," said Les, the bus driver.

"This is Susie," I told him, climbing into the bus behind her.

"Welcome aboard, Susie!"

"Yep!" she said, a little bashful, and slid into the second seat.

"Rachel, sit with me!" she pleaded when I passed her seat.

"Only today," I told her. "I always sit with Kathy."

Kathy and her older sister Luann, who always sat with Kim, got on at the next stop. Carol took a seat by Mona, a high school sophomore, who was already on the bus.

Sixteen more miles over dusty gravel and dirt roads, six more farm stops, and forty minutes later we arrived at school. The gnawing in my stomach returned and my heart beat faster when the bus came to a stop by the opening in the low white fence around the schoolyard. Les opened the door. We filed through the opening of the freshly painted board fence and stepped into a new school year.

3

When I stepped off the bus, my best friends, Melissa and Winnie, were walking on the curved sidewalk in front of the school. A girl I had never seen before was with them.

Must be a new girl. I wonder what class she's in, I thought.

"Rachel, where do I go?" Susie asked, nervous.

"First grade is on this side of the school," I said. We walked across the dry ground with its occasional tufts of grass toward the large double door with BOYS chiseled in the stone over it.

"What does it say above the door, Rachel?"

"'Boys,'" I answered.

"Can *I* go in there?"

"Sure."

"But I'm a girl."

"It doesn't mean anything," I said. "See, Carol and

Mona are going in that door. That's the door all the high schoolers use."

"I'm not in high school."

"Your room is the first one inside the door. That's where the first-grade room is." My voice betrayed my impatience. I was anxious to catch up to Winnie and Melissa and find out about the new girl.

I held open the heavy door for Susie. The brass handle and inside door hardware had been polished to a shiny gold.

"That first door, that's your room, Susie." I pointed to it.

"Where do I go when it's time to go home?"

"The fifth bus. Ours is the fifth bus in line. There are only two behind it. All right?"

"All right." Susie realized I wasn't going any farther and headed for her door with her supplies in hand. She was a small body in the middle of high school bodies streaming by and walking up the stairs to the assembly hall, where each would stake claim to a desk in a particular class section.

A twinge of guilt stung when I saw Susie's small form disappear into her room. I remembered that it *was* her *very first day of school* and realized I hadn't been very nice. But other concerns were on my mind, and the guilt passed as soon as the door closed behind me.

I stepped quickly along the sidewalk, which curved

around the grassy area where the flagpole stood in front of the two-story brick school. The flag's shadow waved slowly on the ground near the giant strikes. The chain clanked against the tall iron pole with its new coat of silver paint. The sun's reflection beamed from the east side of the shiny pole.

I spotted Winnie and Melissa on the curved sidewalk in front of the double door on the other side of the school. GIRLS was carved into the stone above that door. The new girl was with them.

Winnie and Melissa were listening to the new girl, who talked and moved her head in ways that indicated she thought she was important. Her long honey brown ponytail bounced when she talked.

"Hi!" I said as I approached.

"Rachel! Rebecca's in fifth grade!" Winnie said.

She makes it sound like it's the greatest thing in the world, I thought.

"Well, how about that!" I said. I made it sound like a big deal, too.

"Where're you from?" I asked Rebecca.

"She's from Rapid City. Her dad—" Winnie started explaining.

"I'll tell it," Rebecca said. "My dad is boss of the road crew working on Highway 20. Our real home is in Rapid City. That's three hundred miles from here on the edge of the Black Hills."

We all know where Rapid City is, Rebecca!

"We live in a trailer house when Dad works far from home."

"Oh," I replied. I wasn't interested in hearing much more. She had such a superior attitude. Besides, I wanted to see the fifth- and sixth-grade room and pick my seat.

"Did you bring your things up to the room?" I asked Melissa, who was standing beside me.

"Yep. We chose our seats already, too."

That made me anxious to get to the room and see what seats were left. "I'm going up now to choose mine. Want to come with me?"

"Sure," Melissa said. We headed for the door.

"The new girl seems a little bossy and tah-tah," I said.

"Yeah, she does," Melissa agreed.

I opened one side of the heavy double door under the word GIRLS. Its handle and bar and metal edges were polished, too. The smell of new paint and varnish lingered in the building.

We passed by the third- and fourth-grade room, waving briefly through the door to some of the kids we had shared the room with last year. Then we continued down the hall to the stairs. The stucco walls and concrete steps were painted a shiny gray. The wood banisters and the board with the coat hooks on the landing had a new coat of varnish. Melissa and I slowed our pace at the landing. It was warm this September morning and we didn't have coats to hang up.

At the top of the next flight, the door was open to the fifth- and sixth-grade room. I was a little nervous about entering the room and having Mrs. Kelly for a teacher. The older kids had told us that she was strict and that we wouldn't be able to get away with anything in her room.

Mrs. Kelly's desk was by the door, and she was standing beside it. She greeted me with a nice smile and said, "Good morning, Rachel."

"Good morning, Mrs. Kelly," I said.

Her brown eyes were friendly. Her shoulder-length brown hair was pulled back from her face, which was brightened by red lips. Her thin figure looked nice in her navy blue suit.

"Fifth grade is on this side," she said, motioning toward the rows of desks closest to the door. "You can choose any seat that hasn't been taken."

I smiled and nodded. *How could anyone think she was strict?* I wondered.

The room was filled with desks—five rows of them, with six desks in each row. Each row's desk legs were screwed to long thin boards, like they were on train tracks. Those "tracks" allowed the whole row to be moved at once to the side of the room. It was also easier to remove a desk from the boards than from the wood floor, now shiny with a high-gloss varnish.

A few sixth graders were in the room on the side near the windows.

"Are there a lot of new kids?" I asked Melissa.

"Only three that I know of so far. One in sixth and two in fifth."

"Where are you sitting?" I asked.

"Here." She indicated the third desk in the second row.

"Did anyone take this one yet?" I asked, pointing to the desk across from her in the row by the door.

"It's empty, so probably not."

I laid my black notebook on top, put my ink bottle in the round inkwell on the desktop, and put everything away except my yellow pencils.

"Where's Winnie sitting?" I asked.

"Behind me," Melissa answered.

"Rebecca?"

"Beside Winnie."

Behind me, I realized.

I spotted a pencil sharpener by the first window and went over to sharpen my pencils. Out the window, I saw the top of the swings. Last year, it was the sides of the swings we saw from the room beneath.

I laid my sharpened pencils in the pencil groove on my desk. On the very top left of the desk, the initials **DM** were carved and blackened with ink. I swung the hinged seat down and saw **LS** scratched in the smooth wood on the top side of the seat. I wasn't ready to sit down.

The round clock on the wall said 8:50. Five minutes until the bell.

"Who's new besides Rebecca?" I asked Melissa.

"There's Ione in fifth, and her brother Lester is in sixth."

"Is Ione bossy like Rebecca?" I turned my back and mouthed the question in a whisper. I didn't want Mrs. Kelly to hear me.

"I don't know. Haven't seen her yet. I just know what my mom heard downtown."

Loud voices of kids running up the stairs echoed in the hall. Mrs. Kelly crossed to the door and stood in the hall with her arms folded in front of her, waiting for the culprits to appear at the landing.

Melissa and I exchanged someone's-in-for-it glances.

"You go back down those stairs, this minute, and take them one at a time!" Mrs. Kelly's voice was strict. I knew then that I never wanted to do anything to make her scold me like that.

The chatter stopped and footsteps were retraced to the landing. Slow, careful footsteps up the stairs followed.

"That's better!" Mrs. Kelly said.

By now, Melissa and I and the others in the

room were dying to see who it was. Two sheepish, embarrassed faces appeared at the door. It was a boy and a girl we had never seen before.

Melissa and I noticed the same thing when they came into the room. We exchanged slight nods of agreement.

"Cuuute!" I mouthed to her, referring to the boy with his dark hair slicked down.

Melissa nodded again.

"Are you Ione and Lester Fieldman?" Mrs. Kelly asked.

They nodded their heads, fear in their eyes as they looked at her.

"Ione, the fifth grade is on this side. Lester, the sixth on that. You can choose your desks for now," Mrs. Kelly told them in her regular teacher voice.

Ione walked toward me. She paused at the desk in front of me, pointed to it, and asked with her eyes if the desk was available. I nodded and gave her a quick smile. She placed her materials on the desk and quietly sat down.

Her brother chose the front desk by the windows. He was in easy sight from my desk. And Melissa's. She was watching him, too.

4

The bell rang in the hall. It was loud, and I thought that it must be close to our door.

Soon the hall was buzzing with students. Seventh and eighth graders passed our door to their room at the end of the hall. They knew from past experience not to run or use loud voices near Mrs. Kelly's room. Kim waved at me when she went by with her friends.

Winnie, Rebecca, and the rest of the fifth and sixth graders walked into the room and took their seats. There was quiet in the room. We listened for more footsteps while Mrs. Kelly waited by the door.

I caught Winnie's eye and pointed quickly in Lester's direction. Mrs. Kelly had closed the door, so I didn't wait for Winnie's reaction. I gave Mrs. Kelly my attention. So did the others.

"Good morning, boys and girls! A special welcome to the fifth graders!" She nodded in our direction.

Then, including everyone in her gaze, she said, "I hope that all of you had an enjoyable summer, *and*,"—she smiled a sweet, devilish smile—"*and* I hope that now you are ready to work hard and learn as much as possible. Most of the sixth graders had me for their teacher last year and know what I expect of them. And I know that you, fifth graders, will soon know what I expect, also. We begin each day with the pledge, so please rise for the Pledge of Allegiance."

We rose, faced the flag extending from the side of the door frame, and recited the pledge, our right hands across the left side of our chests.

"I think many of you have met our new students," Mrs. Kelly began after the pledge. "Rebecca Carlson. Ione Fieldman. Lester Fieldman." She gestured toward each one.

"Would you like to tell us a little about yourselves?" She looked at Lester, then Ione, then Rebecca.

When she looked at Rebecca, I felt my desk move as Rebecca stood up.

"I'm Rebecca Carlson. My dad is James Carlson, the boss of the gravel crew working on Highway 20." She continued with the same information I had heard on the playground. When she talked about her dad's job, she gave it so much importance.

She thinks her dad's work is so much more important than the rest of our dads', I thought.

"Thank you, Rebecca," Mrs. Kelly said when Rebecca had finished.

"Now, Ione, would you like to tell us about yourself?"

Ione shook her head—small, quick shakes that said, "Absolutely not!"

"Lester?"

Lester shook his head, too, but less emphatically.

At the end of the introductions, Mrs. Kelly said, "Boys and girls, I hope you will make our new students feel welcome."

Mrs. Kelly picked up her pointer and went through the schedule and some important dates written on the side blackboard. The black rubber tip at the end of her wooden pointer touched each line as she talked about it.

The first thing I looked for in the daily schedule was "Recess." We still had three of them, and the noon recess was one hour. "Opening and Pledge" were at 9:00. We had spelling, reading, penmanship, arithmetic, and grammar in the morning. After lunch, the first thing was "Literature Aloud," my favorite thing next to recess. Then history, geography, science, and things like "Weekly Reader," music, and art were in the afternoon. Dismissal was at 3:50.

Mrs. Kelly asked the first person in each row to

help hand out books. David was first in our row and started passing out reading books. He passed by me, anxious to get to Rebecca, I assumed.

"Uuuuh, David." I held out my hand for a book. "Thaaank you!" I said with sarcasm.

I opened the book and smiled when I saw "Carol Johnson" four blanks above where I would write my name under "Student." I recognized all the other names above mine, too. Mrs. Kelly called for our book numbers and wrote them in her grade book. Mine was 10.

The fifth graders had a chance to look through their books while the sixth graders were getting theirs. I watched Lester pass out books to his row after I wrote my name with my best penmanship on the covers of my workbooks for spelling, reading, and grammar.

Finally it was time for recess. The loud bell in the hall would let us know in case we weren't watching the clock. Seventh and eighth graders streamed from their room, mixing with us fifth and sixth graders who hugged the left side of the stairs.

Mrs. Kelly was standing watch by her door. No one ran. Mrs. Kelly and Mrs. Stillman, the seventh- and eighth-grade teacher, followed us outside.

Winnie and Rebecca walked to the swings. Melissa and I followed. All four swings dangled free. With dresses on, we were not interested in real swinging, the kind where we would see if we could get the chains parallel to the top bar. We sat and gently circled the seats above the foot-worn dips scooped out beneath each swing. We wouldn't get our shoes and anklets dusty this way, either.

"I like Mrs. Kelly," I said.

"I do, too, even though she's strict," Winnie said.

"I had the best teacher in the world last year in Rapid City," said Rebecca.

Here we go again, I thought. Then I noticed Ione standing on the sidewalk by the door, shoulders hunched forward.

"I'm going to ask Ione to come over here with us," I said. When no one objected, I ran to her. "Come join us. We're just talking." She followed me to the swings.

"Where'd you go to school last year?" I asked her.

"Huron," she answered.

Our family went to the South Dakota State Fair there each year. But not this year. *I wonder if Rebecca knows that Huron's about seventy miles south and twenty miles east of here.*

"Was school much different there?"

"We had a lot more kids in the school. And only one grade in each room."

"Ione, does *your* dad work on the road, too?" Rebecca asked.

"No, we live on a farm."

"Oh," Rebecca said, as if she were no longer interested.

There it was again. Rebecca's sense of being superior. I felt angry and might have said something, but Melissa asked Ione a question about something more important than *anything* about Rebecca, and I wanted to hear the answer.

"Does Lester have a girlfriend?"

"He had one in Huron. She wrote him a couple of letters this summer."

"I think he's cute," I said.

"Me too," Melissa said.

"I saw him first," I declared.

"*I* saw him first," Melissa claimed.

"Girls always think he's cute," Ione said.

The loud brass bell interrupted our Lester conversation.

5

The rest of our books were passed out after recess. The last book was a new history book for both grades.

Mrs. Kelly took one of the new books and demonstrated the steps of opening and carefully pressing its center in a few places to gently break in its spine.

I paged through the first unit about the Roman Empire. *What funny clothes the men wore in the pictures! Like short dresses,* I thought. I caught Winnie's eye and pointed to the picture of the Roman men. Her eyes widened and she wrinkled her nose.

I wrote my name on the top line under "Student." At the end of the line the word "New" was printed.

"Take good care of your books," Mrs. Kelly reminded us. "Any unnecessary wear or damage will mean a fine when the books are turned in at the end of the year."

I was curious about the Roman Empire and hoped I would be able to take the book home. I raised my hand.

"Yes, Rachel?" Mrs. Kelly said.

"May we take our books home tonight, Mrs. Kelly?"

"Yes, you may."

"Even our new history book?"

"Of course," she answered.

"Any more questions?" Mrs. Kelly paused for a couple of seconds. "If not, the buses will be leaving at eleven-thirty today. In these last minutes, does anyone want to tell about something special that happened this summer?"

Rebecca's hand shot up.

"Rebecca."

"Well, as you know, my dad, mom, and me moved to Cresbard this summer."

I, Rebecca, it's 'My dad, mom, and I moved to Cresbard'! Didn't you learn your grammar in Rapid City from the best teacher in the world? Mrs. Ohlman had drummed that into us during our grammar classes the past two years. *So-and-so and I. She and I. He and I. You and I.*

I tuned in to Rebecca's words again. "We moved our trailer house up here on the edge of town. And one more thing, my mom is going to have a baby. Probably December."

"Rachel has a new baby in her family," Winnie piped up.

"Yes, I heard about that," Mrs. Kelly said. "You turned out to be quite a hero getting your mom to the hospital on time, Rachel. Do you want to tell us about it?"

"Not really. Nothing to tell. I just drove her to the hospital," I said.

"*You* drove her to the hospital?" Rebecca asked.

"No one else was home." I shrugged.

"Wow!"

She's impressed. Rebecca's impressed, I thought.

"Well, boys and girls, it's time to get ready to go," Mrs. Kelly said.

"I'd like you to note the important dates on the side blackboard."

I had already done that. "September 22—School Pictures" was the first date listed. I was glad there were two weeks until I had to worry about that.

"I'll dismiss you by rows when it looks like your row is ready," Mrs. Kelly said. "Don't forget to put up your seat."

I remembered the new history book and quickly removed it from my desk. When Mrs. Kelly called "Row one," I stood and lifted my seat. I had seen how much easier it was for John, our school janitor, to dust the floor when the seats were all up. He had to stop, stoop down, and lift the seats that weren't up.

Mrs. Kelly was standing by the door. She smiled at me when I got there.

"Goodbye, Mrs. Kelly," I said, returning her smile.

"Goodbye, Rachel!"

I walked down the steps with Melissa. Halfway down the stairs, I heard the door of the seventh- and eighth-grade room open and a rush of footsteps behind.

What was their hurry? I wondered. I wasn't in any hurry. I knew that work was waiting for me at home, but I didn't know exactly what.

"Bye, Rachel!" Melissa said when we headed toward different buses.

"Bye, Melissa! See you tomorrow." I quickened my steps, hoping that Susie had found the right bus, since I didn't see her anywhere on the playground.

I was relieved to find Susie in the second seat on the right. The same one she had sat in on the way to school.

"Sit with me, Rachel." She slid over by the window and I sat down. I could sit with Kathy tomorrow, I decided.

"How was school? Your *very* first day?" I asked.

"I love school! And my teacher is nice," Susie said.

"Yeah, I loved Mrs. Bell, too, when I was in first grade," I said, remembering the homey, comfortable feel of my first year of school.

"Mrs. Bell let us pick our own desks. I got one in the front row." Susie talked on but I stopped listening. I was watching the seventh and eighth graders and suave high school kids getting on the bus. Carol, too, looked sophisticated. She and Mona were jabbering on and on about the first day of high school.

When I became aware of a tapping on my arm, I realized Susie had just said, "I had a wonderful *very first day of school!*"

"That's good, Susie."

When all the kids on our route were on the bus, Les swung the handle lever and the door unfolded shut. After a brief grinding of gears, the buses crawled forward like a slow yellow-orange and black train. At the street, some buses turned right, some left. Ours turned right for a block and a half, then left down Main Street, past three blocks of residences, past three blocks of merchants, past the gas station, the implement dealer, grain elevators, and the livestock sale barn at the edge of town. For the next mile, we paralleled an alfalfa field, also used as a landing strip for Kathy's dad's airplane, on the way to Highway 20, where Rebecca Carlson's dad was *boss of the road crew.*

Highway 20 was the north side of our bus route,

mainly a large rectangle with a few detours in or out to drop kids off at their farms. Our farm was a two-mile detour about midpoint on the south side. The detour was one mile south and then one mile east. We referred to the mile east as our "mile road." It's shaped like a question mark because the road curves around a bend in the creek.

Noisy chatter filled the bus during the first several miles. At each farm stop, the chatter lessened by two or three kids.

For most of the ride, I was turned around talking to Kathy, telling her all about Rebecca Carlson and Ione and Lester Fieldman. Susie listened wide-eyed to every word.

When the bus turned onto our mile road, I wondered again what work waited for us. I wondered, too, if Dad would seem troubled about whatever was on his mind.

Halfway around the curve, I saw the red M tractor hitched to the flatbed trailer. My heart sank. Picking rock was this afternoon's work.

6

Blackie was waiting for us at the edge of the cement drive. He wagged his tail and pranced in playful jumps around all of us when we stepped off the bus. We protected our clothes from his paws, but not as vigorously as in the morning.

I waved to Kathy through the bus window. As the bus pulled away, the tractor was in my line of vision, reminding me of the grind ahead.

Mom was standing in the kitchen with Matthew in her arms. At first the commotion of all of us coming into the house and wanting to tell Mom about our first day of school startled him, but he didn't cry.

"Mama, I want to kiss Matthew hello," Susie said.

Mom leaned down so Susie could reach him. Susie gave him a loud smack on his fat baby cheek. Then in that talking-to-baby tone she had heard from adults, she asked, "How are you, Matthew?"

Matthew's face twisted a little and Mom said, "I

think he just gave you another smile, Susie."

"I'm glad to see you too, Matthew, even though I did have a *very* good first day of school," Susie said.

"Yes, everything's right in his world now that his sisters are home," Mom said.

"By the way, any questions, girls, about what you will be doing after you change clothes and eat dinner?" Mom asked, smiling. Her eyes darted through the window to the tractor and trailer parked nearby.

"Picking rock," I said, the dread obvious in my voice.

"Come on, Rachel, picking rock's not so bad, especially if you get to drive the tractor," Kim teased.

I wrinkled my nose at her because I hadn't had a chance to drive the tractor while picking rock yet. Dad allowed Kim and Carol to drive the M, but not me. I was stuck plodding through soft dirt and picking up rocks the whole time.

The smell of food filled the kitchen. Mom had dinner almost ready and the table set. A pan on the stove was spitting steam through its lid. It likely held potatoes cooking for yummy mashed potatoes. A pie with heaping brown-tinged meringue sat on the counter.

"Is that lemon meringue?" I asked.

"Yes, your dad's favorite," Mom said.

"Mine too!" I added.

Another pan sat quietly on another burner. "Beans?" I asked, pointing.

"Nope," Mom answered.

"Peas?"

"No," she said, shaking her head.

"Corn?"

"No."

"Hmm."

"Surprise," Mom said.

"You'd better change your clothes now, girls. Dad will be in soon, so don't dawdle."

We went to our rooms and put on our work jeans and shirts. By the time we were back in the kitchen, Dad was turning on the kitchen radio to hear the farm market report.

Susie was telling him about her very first day of school. I, for one, was glad that she would never have a very first day again.

"And how is your rock-picking arm?" Dad asked Susie.

"Real good. See how good it is, Daddy." She bent her right elbow and lifted her arm to a strong-arm position.

Dad felt her upper-arm muscle and said, "That's good. That's good. But it will be even better after picking up a few rocks."

"Kid?" Mom said softly to Dad. "I'd like to have Susie stay with me and give Matthew some attention. It's been a quiet morning for him."

Dad looked at the little bundle in one-piece terry

cloth pajamas that covered his arms and legs. "Sure," he said. Then again, softly, "Sure."

That look came over Dad's face, like he was in pain. We all noticed it but didn't ask. Just waited, wondering.

"I get to stay with Mama and Matthew?" Susie asked, breaking the silence.

"Yes, you do," Dad said. "We'll work on that rock-picking arm another time."

Dad took his seat at the table. Mom handed Matthew to Carol, reminding her to hold his head. Then she removed the Swiss steak from the oven and placed it on a hot pad in the middle of the table. The potatoes came in a yellow bowl as cut-up pieces. We'd have to mash them ourselves with a fork. A gravy boat with dark brown gravy came next.

"Do you know what's in the other pan?" I leaned over to Kim and asked softly.

She shook her head.

Mom was emptying the other pan into a bowl on the stove. The bar that divided our table from the counter area was too high to see over. Whatever it was, it wasn't something that filled the kitchen with good smells like apples cooking or a roast.

Mom brought a blue serving bowl with a lid and set it by Dad.

"Something special for you, Kid," Mom told Dad and then sat down, taking Matthew from Carol.

"Let's pray," Dad said. "Then I can check what's in this bowl."

I bowed my head, interlocked my fingers, and recited the table prayer with everyone, wondering what was in the bowl by Dad.

". . . and let this food to us be blessed. Amen." All eyes were on Dad and the blue bowl. He lifted the lid and a smile crossed his face. "Thanks, Kid!"

"Spinach!" Kim exclaimed in the same way someone says, "Yuck!" when she saw Dad spoon some onto his plate.

When I saw the limp, wrinkled, dark green stuff, I thought, *"Yuck!"* I'm glad I didn't say it. Kim got the reprimand. "Mind your manners, Kim," Mom warned.

Dad happily spooned half of the spinach onto his plate. He passed the bowl to me on his right. I spooned about two bites onto my plate, careful not to make a face. I was relieved that neither parent insisted I take more.

I felt devilish when I passed the bowl to Kim, daring her with my eyes and smirk to pass it on without taking any. She gave me a dirty look with narrowed eyes and took one small spoonful.

"That's not enough to taste," Dad said. "Take another spoonful."

Kim groaned and took another small spoonful. My smug smile said, "Hah-hah!"

Carol took a small helping and put a little on Susie's plate.

Mom was feeding warm baby cereal to Matthew. He was just starting solid food. Mom fed him with a baby spoon and Matthew worked each creamy spoonful with his tongue and lips for a long time before swallowing about half of it. The rest of it he pushed back out, and it waited on his lips until Mom scraped it up with the spoon and fed it to him for his next bite.

Dad became silent, watching Matthew. That faraway look and sadness had returned.

"Dad?" I said.

He blinked his eyes, indicating that he was back from that distant place to the table in our kitchen.

"Yes, Rachel?" He surprised me with a response.

I had wanted to ask, "What's the matter?" but it didn't feel right, so I answered, "Oh, nothing."

Before Dad left the table, he said, "The spinach was a real treat, Kid." Then he added, shaking his head, "These days, kids don't know what's good for them.

"But I know what's good for them," he teased. "Hard work. And it's time to get at it."

How I wished I had a choice in the matter!

7

Dad started the tractor and let it idle. Carol, Kim, and I jumped on the edge of the flatbed wagon, our legs dangling over the side. Dad shifted into low gear, let out the clutch, and opened the throttle to pick up speed. The empty trailer bounced over each small bump on the trail leading behind our farm to the alfalfa field Dad had plowed.

When Dad shifted to second, the bumps came harder and more often. I almost bounced off the wagon from one bump. Before he shifted to third, I pulled my legs onto the trailer bed and moved closer to the middle.

"Are you . . . oo staying there . . . ere?" I asked Carol and Kim. Each bump cut my words into staccato parts.

"Yeah . . . eah," Kim said. "The mid . . . id . . . dle is just for . . . or sissies."

"Whoa!" Dad exclaimed. The front wagon wheel

hit a big bump and the wagon bounced high, throwing Carol and Kim off balance. Dad couldn't stop the tractor before the rear of the wagon bounced high, too, knocking Carol and Kim off.

I was afraid that they might have been hurt.

"Are you girls all right?" Dad asked from the tractor, now at a standstill.

"Yeah," they answered, getting up and shaking the grass from their clothes.

"I didn't see that badger hole," he called back in apology.

"Slow down a little!" Carol told him, irritated. "It's awful bumpy on this wagon."

"Yeah," Kim scolded.

Both sat by me in the middle this time.

"I guess this sissy spot isn't so bad after all," I said to Kim real fast before Dad started moving again.

Blackie trailed along behind us and to the side of us, his nose sniffing the ground for hints of prey. The badger hole held his attention. He sniffed around it and dug into it, then backed out and followed us again.

The freshly plowed alfalfa field was only a quarter mile from home, so we didn't have to bounce around on the wagon much longer. It was an old alfalfa field and Dad said it was time to plow it under so we could plant corn there next year.

At the edge of the field, the dark brown earth

stretched ahead for a quarter of a mile.

At the corner of the field, Dad shifted into low gear. We jumped off the wagon and spread out over the plowed ground. Kim and I walked on one side of the wagon, Carol on the other. We scanned the soil for rocks, which we picked up and placed on the wagon. The wagon didn't bounce in the loose soil, so the rocks didn't fall off.

"Where do these rocks come from?" I complained, surprised at all the solid lumps in the loose brown soil. "Every year we pick up rocks from the dirt fields and we pick up every rock we see. Where do they all come from?"

"Are you talking to me?" Kim asked. "You might as well be talking to the man in the moon, because I'm not listening."

She leaned over and picked up a light gray rock. Most of the rocks would be small—the size of two, three, four fists, large enough to break parts of farm machinery. They weighed five, ten, fifteen pounds. "Easier for kids to run after than an old man with back problems," Dad explained after Carol asked why he got to drive the tractor all the time and we had to do the hard work.

While watching Kim pick up her rock, I stubbed my toe on a black one. It was a stubborn rock, didn't want to be moved from its warm bed in the soft earth. I plopped down on my knees and worked my fingers under the sides in the soil to loosen it.

The tractor and wagon moved on. I worked harder to get the rock so I wouldn't have to run with it so far to the wagon. Finally it came loose. It was heavy, and I was panting hard by the time I caught up to the wagon.

The rock clunked on the wagon's boards. Without the dirt cradling it, the rock looked like a sperm whale.

The wagon moved on and I fanned out across the dirt. The next rock in my path was green and shaped like a closed clam. *What is this? A sea?* Then I knew. *It's a sea of soil.* I placed the clam rock by the whale rock.

It sure would be fun to find a rock shaped like a sea horse, I thought, heading toward a light-colored rock I had spotted. I crossed Kim's sunken footprints to get to it.

This rock was not a sea creature. Light gray with small dark spots, it was shaped like a dried cowpie, as though the rock had once been runny and then dried layer on top of layer. I was glad it wasn't the same color as a cowpie.

"Hey, Rachel! Pick up the rock! Don't just look at it!" Kim yelled to me. The tractor and wagon had moved some distance ahead.

I picked up the rock with its tiered edges and ran to catch up with the wagon. Kim had piled rocks around my whale and clam rocks. Disappointed, I tossed this one on top of the heap.

Rocks were piling up on Carol's side, too.

The tractor and wagon tires pressed trails in the ground. The small front tractor tires squeezed a small ridge of dirt between them. The large rear tractor tires made wide, deep, incomplete Vs. Straight lines alternating with wavy lines were made by the wagon. Branching out from the tire tracks were our footprints, of three slightly different sizes and depths. Blackie's pawprints zigzagged across the dirt to the edge of the plowed field, where he ran with his nose to the ground.

"Whoa!" Dad exclaimed, and stopped the tractor. He got off and helped pick rocks. "They're like mushrooms in this spot!" he said.

We picked all sizes, shapes, and colors there. Some pink, some green, reddish, shades of gray to black, some mixed.

I picked up a black one with shiny gold flecks. "Look!" I showed Carol, who was near. "It looks like a rock with gold in it."

"Fool's gold!" she said.

I thought she was mocking me.

"That's what it's called. Fool's gold," she repeated.

Blackie returned from his sniffing rounds, panting. "You're such a pretty dog for a collie mutt," I told him, carrying a rock. He accepted the compliment with a wag of his tail. It took a big grunt to get the rock up on the wagon.

I smoothed the black fur on Blackie's head. Gratitude and loyalty shone in his brown dog eyes. Of all us kids, I paid the most attention to him. Carol didn't care to have him around her. Kim tolerated him. Susie liked him too, but I was outside more than she was, so Blackie preferred me.

Blackie would follow Dad around but not too close. Dad would yell bad words at him if he ever caught him near the cattle. New cattle spooked easily, so Dad never wanted Blackie in the cattle yards. When cattle get nervous and frightened, they can run right through most fences.

"Rachel!" Dad's call startled me. "This would be a good time to learn how to drive the M," he said. "Come on up here." He motioned to the tractor seat.

"Me?"

"Yeah. Come on. The rocks are picked in this spot. Time to move on."

"Will I get to drive today?" Kim asked.

"We'll see how Rachel does," replied Dad.

8

I was nervous about driving the big M for the first time. I drove the smaller Ford Ferguson all the time. Carol and Kim drove the M and the H tractors.

It was a stretch for my legs to climb from the hitching bar to the tractor seat. The seat was big and padded, instead of metal like the Ford's.

Dad stood on the hitching bar behind me and held on to the seat. "First thing, push in the clutch," he said. The tractor was idling, so I didn't have to turn the key to start it. The clutch was hard to push in. I stretched my leg as far as I could to push it in all the way.

It took a few tries and a lot of gear grinding before I got the hang of shifting gears and letting out the clutch without killing the motor. I was nervous on the high tractor seat with so much machine under me.

"That should be a good speed," Dad said after I

was driving a ways. "Just steer straight ahead." He stepped off the tractor while it was moving.

I was driving the M myself. *My very first day of driving the M,* I thought, mimicking Susie.

I steered straight ahead. That wasn't hard. At one point, Kim ran ahead on her side of the tractor. I was feeling good about driving the M, and when she looked in my direction, I gave her a little smart-aleck wave. She wrinkled her nose at me.

When I reached the end of the field, I turned and turned the steering wheel, proud of the tractor's response.

"Craa . . . ack!" The sound of splintering wood burst behind me. I turned around.

"The clutch! Push in the clutch!" Dad yelled. The big rear tire was ripping the corner of the wagon. I pushed on that clutch with all my might. My rear end was half off the seat to push it all the way in and stop the tractor.

"Turn off the tractor!" Dad ordered.

I reached toward the key with my right hand and felt the pull against my clutch leg. *Oh boy! I can't let this clutch slip!* I thought. I reached through the steering wheel instead of around it and managed to turn off the tractor.

"Whoa! Look at this!" Dad exclaimed, surveying the damage. "You turned too short, Rachel!" he said, shaking his head at me.

"I didn't know," I answered meekly, still pressing the clutch in with all my might.

Carol and Kim came to see. Kim moved her right index finger back and forth over her left index finger, which meant, "Naughty, naughty, shame on you."

"Appears to be just damage to the wood," Dad said, checking the wagon corner. He had calmed down a little. "The tongue and axle look okay." He sounded relieved.

"Let's see if we can get this wagon unhitched," he said. He tried to pull the hitching bolt out of the hole, but it wouldn't budge.

It dawned on me that I still had the clutch pressed in. I took my foot off it but stayed in the tractor seat, out of the way.

"Carol, bring the hammer!" Dad ordered, because she was closest to the toolbox on the side of the tractor. She brought it on the run.

It took several pounds of the hammer before the bolt was up and could be pulled out. Dad dropped the wagon tongue on the ground and put the bolt in an empty hitching-bar hole.

"I'll take over," Dad said. After I climbed down, Dad started the tractor, turned the front wheels in the opposite direction, and put the tractor in gear. He drove it away from the wagon. A few pieces of wood and several rocks fell to the dirt under the smashed corner.

"Hitch me up, Carol!" Dad said, backing the tractor to the tongue.

Kim had to help her straighten the stubborn tongue because the wheels were weighted so heavily with the rock load.

"Can all three of you ride on the bar?" Dad asked, after the wagon was hitched.

"I'll walk," I said.

Dad opened the throttle and the tractor pulled the wagon ahead, widening the brown sea between us. I watched until they passed through the gate to the pasture where the creek had been dammed. The rocks would be tossed along the banks to reinforce the sides of the road across the dam.

Blackie walked beside me. I patted his head, grateful for his company.

"I had my very first day of driving the M today, Blackie." He looked up at me and we kept walking. "I didn't do very well."

We walked across the field, girl and dog prints trailing behind us in irregular parallel.

When I reached the corner of the field nearest home, I remembered that it was the spot where Blackie had saved my life eight years ago.

"You are some dog, Blackie. Besides being pretty—well, handsome, because you're a boy—you are a hero, a lifesaver." Blackie accepted the praise and enjoyed the stroking of his head and neck.

I've heard Mom and Dad tell the story on more than one occasion. Mom was milking cows shortly after we moved to South Dakota from Iowa. I was two years old and had wandered off to the field where Dad was plowing. When Dad stopped plowing to go home for something and was about to get into the pickup, Blackie started barking. He kept barking. That was not typical, so Dad decided to check on the other side of the pickup. That's when he found me barefoot, asleep, against the rear wheel.

Mom and Dad are still amazed that I could have walked that quarter mile of hayfield with tiny bare feet. Walking along with Blackie now, I shuddered at the thought of how that would hurt even my toughened ten-year-old feet.

"They say if you hadn't been barking, I would have been run over. Much obliged, Blackie!" I said, using Dad's way of saying thank you to adults.

I knew one thing, Dad wasn't much obliged to me today.

9

At school, I was able to forget my home troubles. The first week was great. But the second week, there were some disappointments.

Tuesday, Mrs. Kelly said that the boys could not pump the girls on the swings. The girls would sit on a swing's board seat and the boys would stand with their feet on the outsides of the seat. Then they'd pump the swing high in the air. They'd compete to see who could pump the highest. Most of the boys wanted Melissa because she was the smallest girl. Probably because she was the prettiest, too.

Sometimes the boys would get the swing chains as high as the top frame bar. Lance did once with me. The chains were straight out from the top. Boy, did my stomach tickle on that downhill ride! I shrieked, too, which surprised me, because I'm usually a pretty brave girl.

Swinging wasn't much fun after Mrs. Kelly forbade that. She just said, "There will be no more swinging of boys and girls on the same swing." No one dared ask why.

It seemed that Melissa had won the affections of the new boy, Lester. He looked at her a lot during class time and teased her during recess.

And just when I was getting to like Rebecca, her dad was injured and they had to move back to Rapid City.

Then on Wednesday, on our review multiplication facts test, I skipped a whole row of facts—ten on a page of fifty.

For the test, we were to align a sheet of notebook paper under the book's first row of facts, and write only the answers on that paper. After we finished a row, we would fold the answers under so we had a blank line for the next row. In my hurry to be the first one done, I skipped row three. Mrs. Kelly's eyes lit up when I raised my hand, the signal that I was done. She wrote "1:30" on the board, for one minute and thirty seconds. My best speed ever.

Later, when I unfolded my paper to exchange with Melissa, I noticed I had only four rows, not five. My hand shot up.

"Rachel?" Mrs. Kelly said.

"I skipped a whole row, Mrs. Kelly!"

"That's too bad, but they will have to be checked wrong." Her decision dashed my hopes for best speed in the class.

When Mrs. Kelly read the answers to row three, I heard Melissa's pencil check each time.

Melissa had a perfect paper with a time of 1:40. Probably the fastest in the class, unless Winnie or Darren Rennard did better.

When she returned my paper, Melissa gave me a sympathetic smile. Written in her neat handwriting at the top was "–10." I had all the others right.

Melissa did have the best time. Darren had one wrong with a 1:35 time. Lance had checked it wrong. He couldn't tell whether it was a zero or a nine.

When Darren appealed to Mrs. Kelly, she said, "No. The problem was 'zero times nine' and the check mark will stay because students often write 'nine' as the answer, confusing the question with 'zero plus nine.'"

I vowed that for the next timed test, I would have a perfect paper *and* the best time. I had an idea, and it wouldn't be very hard to succeed. I would take my arithmetic book home every night that week and practice my special method.

At home that night, Mom and Dad were quiet. They had received a letter in the mail from our minister, the Reverend Clarence Meyer, apologizing that he would have to postpone Matthew's baptism the next Sunday because his father in Minnesota was gravely ill. We didn't have a phone, so he couldn't call. This was very upsetting to Mom and Dad.

10

Despite the disappointments in school, I was feeling pretty good by the time school was out on Thursday. A donkey basketball game was scheduled for that night in the school gym. We girls could go, and that would be fun.

I had seen a donkey baseball game a couple of years ago at the town baseball diamond. All the action took place on donkeys. The donkeys would get stubborn and refuse to run to the bases with their riders. If the riders kicked the donkeys in the sides to make them move, they'd stand a good chance of getting bucked off.

When the bus drove down Main Street on the way home, I noticed that our pickup was parked in front of the pool hall. *Dad must be playing cards,* I thought.

Dad wasn't home yet when the bus dropped us off

about 4:30. Mom asked, "Did you see Dad's pickup in town, girls?"

"It was parked by the pool hall," I said.

Mom had a worried look on her face. "He's usually home by this time," she said.

Susie, who was hugging and kissing Matthew, stopped and asked, "Do you think something's wrong, Mama?"

"I hope not."

"Here he comes, Mom!" Carol had seen the sun's reflection on the windshield of Dad's pickup when he turned the mile corner. We looked out the window and saw the dust trail behind the pickup.

"He's driving kind of slow," Kim said.

The worry lines deepened on Mom's forehead as she checked the pickup's progress. "We'll soon know what's what," she said.

It seemed a long wait until the red International was parked on the garage driveway.

"He's walking slow," Kim reported, watching from the corner kitchen window.

I looked over her shoulder. "He looks like he's sore from something. Maybe his back hurts him," I said.

The breezeway door opened and shut. Susie went down the kitchen stairs to greet Dad. "Hi, Daddy!"

"Hi, Susie. How was school today?" Dad's speech sounded slower than normal.

"Good!" Susie said.

Dad sat on the upholstered folding chair to take off his boots. The chair squeaked a little.

Mom had a puzzled look on her face. She was waiting in the kitchen work area. She had put Matthew on his tummy on a blanket in the living room.

I waited by the pantry door. Carol and Kim were waiting there, too.

"Hi, Kid!" Dad said when he walked into the kitchen. He had a silly grin on his face. His voice was slow. His steps were slow. His eyes looked different.

"You're drunk!" Mom cried. Her disgust leaped into every corner of the kitchen and into the living room, where Matthew started to fuss. "In front of your children! How could you?"

Drunk! Fear seized me. I had heard of drunk men coming home and beating their wives.

Then another realization hit Mom. "What if you had had an accident? Killed yourself? Or someone else? Oh, Kid, how could you do this?" She turned her back to him, shaking her head, shoulders slumped.

I had never seen Dad drunk before. I had never seen anyone drunk, but the stories I had heard scared me.

Dad walked toward the living room.

"Carol, pick up Matthew," Mom ordered. "We don't want his *father* stumbling on him."

"Come on, now . . . Kid," Dad managed to reply.

He left the kitchen and sat in his rocking chair.

Susie hugged Mom. I was fixed to the same spot in despair. Kim shook her head in disbelief. Carol picked up Matthew and shot a disgusted glance in Dad's direction before coming to the kitchen.

Mom comforted Susie for a minute. Then she filled the coffeepot and plugged it in. She shook her head sadly. Soon, staccato "perks" tried to escape the pot, but the lid held them captive.

No one moved much. I glanced at Dad, sitting quietly in his rocking chair, his hands together with fingers interlocked, like when we say grace before meals.

"Rachel, would you get a can of tomato soup from the pantry, please?" Mom asked. "We'll have tomato soup and grilled cheese sandwiches for supper. Might as well get that started."

I opened the pantry door beside me and got the family-size can of tomato soup. Mom got the Velveeta from the refrigerator and the loaf of Old Home bread from the top of the refrigerator. She asked Kim to put the slices of cheese between two pieces of bread. Mom browned both sides of the sandwiches in a bit of bacon grease in the frying pan until the cheese was soft and hot.

When the coffeepot stopped perking, Mom poured the steaming brown liquid into a cup and carried it to Dad. "Drink this," she said.

"Okay, Kid," he said meekly.

I was standing close to the living room doorway. Dad wasn't acting like the vicious monsters I had heard about. He was just sitting there.

"How do you get drunk?" Susie whispered to me.

"From drinking too much whiskey," I whispered back.

We both looked into the living room at Dad. He took a sip of his coffee and set the cup on the lamp table by his chair.

"Where did he get whiskey?" Susie said, still whispering.

"At the pool hall."

"How's he going to get better?"

"Ask Mom."

Mom was turning the cheese sandwiches. Kim was stirring the soup to keep it from sticking to the pan.

"Mom?" Susie asked softly, over by the stove. "How is Dad going to get over being drunk?"

"After he drinks some coffee and eats something and sleeps, he should be better, honey.

"Set the table please, Rachel," she told me. I took six plates and six soup bowls from the cupboard and set them on the table. Next, I put a tablespoon for the soup and a fork and knife to the right of each plate.

Snoring from the living room halted our movements. We all moved to the doorway. Dad's head rested on the back of his rocker, his eyes closed.

Mom released a sigh. "We'll go ahead and eat, girls. Let him sleep. He can eat later."

Mom poured soup into all the bowls except Dad's. She reserved a bowl for him in the pan. She brought the sandwiches, cut diagonally, to the table. We said grace in soft voices and ate slowly.

Mom looked sad. She held Matthew on her shoulder, her cheek against his, stroking his back, stopping now and then to take a bite of her sandwich.

Kim and Carol don't seem very worried about this, I thought.

"Do you think Matthew knows Dad is drunk?" Susie asked in her loud little-kid voice.

"Not so loud, Susie. We don't want to wake your dad," Mom said.

"Does he?" Susie whispered.

"No. But I'm sure he can sense that all is not normal," Mom answered.

It was a sober meal. Dad's snoring made more noise than our talking.

After the dishes were finished, I heard Kim ask Carol on the way to their room, "What are you wearing?"

Wearing? They can't be thinking of going to the donkey basketball game after this. I followed them into their room and shut the door. "You're not still going, are you?" I asked in a low voice. Dad's rocking chair was just on the other side of the arched doorway outside their room.

"Why not?" Carol said.

"Dad! He might hurt Mom!" I was yelling at them in a whisper.

Kim opened their door and pointed to Dad. "Does he look like he's going to hurt anyone?"

"But when he wakes up," I insisted, closing the door.

"It'll be okay, Rachel," Carol assured.

"Drunk men get violent!" I cried.

"He's not going to get violent," Kim said. "Now go! Get ready."

"I'm not going." I shook my head in disbelief. "Someone has to stay home and protect Mom."

11

Carol, Kim, and Susie went off to the donkey basketball game.

I wasn't taking any chances with Dad's condition. I was possessed with such fear that I wasn't even upset about missing the game. Fear even overcame any anger toward Dad.

I didn't go to my room. I hung around the kitchen. I swept the kitchen floor for Mom. From the living room, Dad snored off and on like he had a snoring switch.

Mom fed Matthew his last bottle in the kitchen. His sucking noises were quiet. The only other sounds were snoring from the living room and the hum of the electric refrigerator motor. Mom burped Matthew and held him over her shoulder until he went to sleep. After a while, she walked softly to her bedroom and laid him in his crib.

I got a dust cloth and wiped the top of the heating registers along the kitchen floor. I wiped slowly. There wasn't much dust. I finished the long register and stood up to do the one on the wall behind the table when a shadow moved on the gray glass wall. In the reflection, I saw Dad behind me.

I turned.

"Where's Mom?" he asked.

"Wh . . . why?"

"I need to talk to her."

I shrugged my shoulders.

I heard Mom quietly close her bedroom door, and then she was in the kitchen behind Dad.

What will he do when he faces her? I thought. My heart raced in fear.

"Kid . . ." Dad's voice was gentle.

"I know," Mom said. "Would you like some tomato soup or a cheese sandwich?" she asked him.

"I know"! What does Mom mean—"I know"?

"I could use something to eat," Dad said. His voice sounded grateful.

I stood with the dust cloth still in my hand, puzzled.

"Are you finished dusting the registers, Rachel?" Mom asked. "When you finish that, you can go read."

I didn't feel like reading, but I could tell that Mom wanted to talk to Dad alone. I wiped the last register, put the dust cloth on top of the vacuum cleaner handle in the pantry, and went to my room.

I left the door open halfway.

I heard Mom heat Dad's soup and sandwich. When she served them, she sat down at the table with him. Mom's voice was too soft to hear from the bedroom, so I crept into the hall and crouched by the kitchen arch.

"You have to do something about this, Kid. It's causing you to do things you usually don't do. Things that can be dangerous. It scares me."

Dad slurped a spoonful of soup. Then there was quiet.

Now I'll find out what's been bothering him. I waited for his reply.

"You're right, Kid. I have to do something about this. It's breaking my heart. Eating away at me."

I waited to hear more, waited to hear what was breaking his heart, but all I heard was Dad eating his soup. He ate it slowly. Sadly, I could tell, and never said another word until he was done eating. Then he said, "Thank you, Kid."

I slipped back into my bedroom when I heard them get up from the table. They went to the living room. The leather seat of Dad's rocking chair squished when he sat down and squeaked when he leaned back.

Mom washed the soup and sandwich dishes before she joined Dad in the living room. Then I heard her paging through a magazine.

Their sounds were quiet, calm, not what I had imagined. Still, I kept an ear tuned to the living room, even though it seemed that they were finished with their serious discussion for the evening.

12

The next big event at school was Picture Day. I decided to wear my good cowboy boots, my cowboy shirt with the mother-of-pearl snaps, and western jeans. Most years I wore the new dress that I had worn on the first day of school. But this year I felt like showing off my new boots, dark brown with fancy black leaf swirls on the tops.

Mom did a double take and said, "Oh!" when I came to the breakfast table. Then she nodded her approval, adding, "Why not?" Dad seemed pleased.

"Can I wear mine, too?" Susie asked.

"You look pretty just like that, Susie," Mom said. She did. Her pageboy curled just right. She was wearing her new school dress.

Kim and Carol were all dressed up in their new skirts and blouses.

Most years Mom would give us home perms before school started. But with baby Matthew, she didn't have time. So none of us had curly hair without a lot of trouble.

I had put curls in my hair with bobby pins before I went to bed the night before. I ended up with big springy curls on top and had to smooth and clamp them down with a barrette. Not exactly what I had had in mind, but my blue cowboy shirt with wavy dark blue lines and fancy snap pockets made up for my hair, I thought.

"Where's your horse, young lady?" Les asked when I stepped up into the bus.

I smiled and answered, "I don't think you'd want him in here."

The only horse we had was a Shetland pony with hooves so long he hobbled. I heard Dad say Pokey was foundered. Dad would try and cut his hooves, but Pokey wouldn't stand still. The last time I tried to ride him, he kicked me in the jaw and knocked me senseless for a couple of minutes. My jaw was black-and-blue for a week.

Pokey was a far cry from Dad's regal black stallion, Midnight. Dad loved horses, but the farm work left him little time to ride, and Midnight had to be rebroken each time. He was too spirited for us kids to ride. Finally Dad sold him because he chased the cattle and we didn't have an extra pasture or pen for him.

I was anxious to get to school and see how my classmates looked. I chuckled when I met Lance on the sidewalk. His front hair was sticking straight up, like a high butch.

He looked at my boots and wrinkled his nose. "Boots? Cowboy boots?" he mocked.

First I was hurt. Then I was angry. "Well, that shows all *you* know!" I snapped. "Since I'm a girl and these boots are on me, wouldn't that make them cow*girl* boots?"

"There isn't such a thing as cow*girl* boots," he declared.

"There is now!" I tromped off, my cowgirl boot heels clumping with every determined step.

I saw Winnie and Melissa by the door. Both were wearing new dresses and their hair was curled in ringlets. Winnie's brown ringlets reached the tops of her shoulders. She had her hair parted in the middle, with a barrette on each side to keep her hair out of her eyes. Melissa's golden curls fell to the middle of her back. Her top hair was pulled back with a barrette, where a cluster of curls bunched together. Her blond hair glistened in the sun. Her eyes were big and clear blue like the sky. When she smiled, big dimples formed in the middle of her cheeks. Her picture would be perfect.

"Neat cowboy boots, Rachel!" Winnie said.

"Thanks, but call them cow*girl* boots in front of Lance, because he made fun of them." I mimicked Lance's "Cowboy boots?" remark for them.

"What does Lance know anyway?" Winnie said, dismissing his opinion.

The bell rang and we entered through the GIRLS door and climbed the stairs with the rest of our class. Most of us were a little self-conscious about being dressed up. The boys teased each other about their slicked-down or waxed-up hair.

Lance decided it was necessary to point out my cowboy boots. "Hey, you guys. Did you see Rachel's cowboy boots? Oh excuse me—cow*girl* boots!"

"Lance, go take a look in the mirror," Winnie said, all serious. "There's something funny on your face."

"What?" he asked, concerned.

"Your nose!" she said, laughing.

He stuck his tongue out at her.

"Good one, Winnie!" I congratulated her.

"How can you stand those two?" Lance asked Melissa.

Melissa shrugged and gave him a dimpled smile.

"Too bad you girls aren't nice like Melissa," Lance said.

Mrs. Kelly was at the door, holding it open for the kids as she did each morning. I think she stood there because she could keep her eye on us at the coat hooks on the landing.

"You're a little noisy down there," she reprimanded.

We quit the banter immediately and walked into the room.

When it was our class's turn for pictures, Mrs. Kelly let us go to the bathroom to comb our hair and check our clothes. We jockeyed for turns in the two mirrors above the sinks.

My hair still looked ridiculous. I took out the barrette and tried to flatten the springy curls a little, but others sprang up in a different place, so I redid it the way it was.

Melissa stood back. She didn't have to fix her hair. Her curls were exactly where her mother had fixed them that morning.

In the gym, Mrs. Kelly lined us up shortest first. I was near the front, between Melissa and Lance. Lance couldn't tease me because Mrs. Kelly was standing near us.

Each of us took a turn sitting on a stool with a blue backdrop behind it. When Melissa sat down, her long blond ringlets glowed in the light. The blue backdrop made her big eyes even bluer. The dimples deepened when she smiled, and there were no spaces between her front teeth.

I was next. "Look right at me," the photographer said. "Chin up a little. Now smile."

I smiled, keeping my lips together.

"Come on. You can do better than that," he coaxed.

I stretched my smile but kept my lips closed.

"Glued your lips together this morning, did you?" he joked.

My answer was a laugh with a wide-open smile. The shutter clicked faster than I could close my mouth.

My hopes for a good picture this year were ruined.

I wasn't in a good mood when our class posed for the group picture. I sat near the middle of those on chairs, another third stood behind the chairs, and the others stood on chairs in the back row. Lester, I noticed, stood behind Melissa.

When the photographer said, "Say cheese," I barely smiled, my lips closed.

13

The next Saturday morning, I had some free time for a change. Dad had gone to town for repairs on the pickup. Carol, Kim, and I finished feeding hay to the cattle, and no other chores had been assigned, so our time was our own. Susie was in the house, entertaining Matthew to help Mom.

It was a beautiful late September morning. The air was crisp with the promise of warmth when the sun rose higher. It was dry, and no dew collected on my boots.

I decided to walk to the junk pile in the pasture. Blackie came along. I climbed the wooden gate. Blackie took a running leap and cleared the top barbed wire of the fence with a few inches to spare.

I followed the tire tracks to the junk pile on the sloping bank of the creek. An old threshing machine, dark reddish brown from years of rusting, and an old horse-drawn dump rake the same color stood sentry on one end of the heap of discarded things.

I stopped by the rake and touched the large iron wheel. I was tempted to sit in its high seat just for fun, but I knew reddish brown powder would cling to the seat of my pants. I had already darkened the front legs of my jeans when I wiped the rust from my hands on them.

Only once had I seen a dump rake drawn by horses, and that was a few years ago, when our neighbors Otto and Jesse Harmon were still farming with horses. Instead of making windrow rectangles around a field, the windrows were straight lines—all parallel with each other. The rake dragged the cut hay to the windrow line, where Otto tripped the rake to dump the hay. Then he continued across the field, dragging hay and tripping the rake at the windrow lines. There was no hurry, just a steady pace of dragging and tripping.

I followed a worn, dusty cow path that wound around the junk pile and then turned toward the creek. Blackie continued along the path, his nose to the ground. I doubted that he would follow it all the way to the far end, where the cattle gathered to drink and cool off in the creek at a low spot. I was glad to see that the cattle were that far away now.

My interest was the big heap where old broken things had been tossed over the years. I stepped on a bed of rusted iron springs to get to the middle of the pile. Underneath the springs were rusted tin cans without labels. Small cans, the size of tuna cans, larger ones the size of vegetable cans. Glass jars—pints, quarts, half-gallon, and gallon jars—were all over, many broken. Milk bottles, whole and broken.

I recognized the old green chamber pot from our bedroom in the old house. I shuddered at the memory of only cold running water and no bathroom.

The familiar handle of my old red scooter poking through the top of the pile caught my eye. How much fun I had had gathering speed with my running foot and then coasting until the scooter stopped, each time trying to go farther than before on the cement drive and sidewalk.

I stepped on the bowl of the old cream separator and pulled the scooter from the pile. Old cans and jars dropped away as the frame emerged, slightly bent, with the footboard missing. A few patches of red paint remained on the rusted metal. The small tires were still good, but the white hubs were pockmarked with rust.

I looked for the footboard beneath a broken chair and some broken dishes in that spot, but no luck. I scouted over the pile, testing each step before putting my full weight on it. When I got to the edge, I scoured the rim for signs of the footboard.

Blackie's nose had led him off the cow path and back to the pile. Under the pile somewhere must be a gopher with a racing heartbeat. *Maybe even cowering behind my old scooter footboard,* I thought with a smile.

I crisscrossed the pile in the other direction but didn't find the footboard.

Tiring of the search, I followed the cow path down to the creek. Hundreds of minnows were streaking around in the shallow water close to the bank. A water strider was showing off its ability to walk on water.

I picked up a rock and threw it as far out as I could, hoping it would plunk down in the middle of the wide creek. It splashed just short of the middle. I watched each new ripple chase the wave before it farther from the point where the rock broke water.

I tossed a pebble a few feet from the water strider, curious to see how it would ride the waves. It held steady, rocking back and forth on its wave.

A big rock jutted from the grass several feet ahead. I yearned for a big splashing! It took muscle to lift the rock over my head and plunge it into the water, deeper at this point near the bank.

"Kerplunk!" I watched large water drops splash back into the disturbed water. Muddy half-circle ripples rolled away from the bank. The minnows and water strider were gone. For a while, I watched the mud settle back to the creek bottom.

When I turned to retrace my steps up the cow path,

I was stunned by the white face staring at me from the top of the bank. One of the new Hereford heifers Dad had bought in Lemmon, west of the Missouri River, stood watching me. I thought that all the cattle were at the far end of the pasture when I had climbed the gate.

"Blackie?" I yelled when I didn't see him. He came running from the far side of the junk pile.

"Stay by me, boy!" I commanded.

The heifer stood her ground. I felt cornered.

"Sic her, Blackie!" I yelled. Blackie shot up the steep bank, barking at the heifer. She hesitated, lowered her head at him, then turned and ran away.

I raced up the bank to see how far she had gone. She was a hundred yards from me and still running in the other direction.

Blackie circled back to me. "Sic her, Blackie! Sic her!" I commanded again, not because I thought it was necessary. I enjoyed watching Blackie scare her. And I was taking revenge for the scare she had given me.

He obediently chased after her, barking. The heifer ran faster. When Blackie caught up to her, she turned and ran toward the fence.

Good grief! What is she doing? I thought. *With all that pasture out there, why is she running toward the fence?*

She gained momentum and I watched in horror as

she jumped over the fence. She almost cleared it, but her hind foot caught the top strand of barbed wire. A *twaing* rang out when the strained wire snapped. The heifer stumbled and then ran along the outside of the fence.

Blackie was about to take a running leap over the fence after her.

"No, Blackie! Here, boy! Come here!"

He ran to me. My heart raced from fear at the thought of what I had just caused.

"Oh, Blackie! Dad is not going to like this."

My stomach became a knot. It would be difficult to get the heifer back into the pasture. Then the fence would have to be fixed. I prayed that Dad would not ask how it had happened.

The truth would mean trouble for me. And so would a lie.

14

I kept track of the heifer. She had gone through the open gate to the plowed field where we had picked rock. She turned the corner and was running along the east fence of the pasture toward the cows grazing there.

I was waiting for Dad when he drove into the yard. "Dad, there's a heifer out!" I gulped.

"Where is she?" Dad asked.

"She's running on the outside of the east pasture fence on this side of the creek." I pointed in that direction.

"Jump in! We'll see if we can get her back in."

Blackie ran beside the pickup.

"Blackie's not going to be of any help. He'll scare her," Dad said.

I rolled my window down and yelled to Blackie, "Go home, Blackie!" He stopped running and stood watching us. I saw his image become smaller in my rear-view mirror.

Driving along the fence, Dad saw the broken wire. "Looks like this is where she went over," he said. I held my breath, fearing the dreaded question, but he didn't ask. He sped off to the gate into the plowed field. Tools in the back clanged at every bump.

"There she is!" I pointed to the heifer in the far corner where our fence line met our neighbor's. She was trying to rejoin the herd in our pasture. She made attempts to push through the woven wire, but the fence held fast. At the corner, she turned around and retraced her steps.

"We'll open the corner gate and try to turn her back toward it," Dad said. He drove to the end of the grass road along the fence, jumped out, and opened the wire gate. He was in a hurry and didn't want to wait for me to struggle with it.

"I hope we can turn her around before she gets to that open gate on the other end!" Dad said. He stepped on the gas pedal, shifted quickly into second, and made a loop in the plowed dirt to get ahead of the heifer.

The heifer became agitated when she saw the pickup heading toward her. She turned and pushed at the fence. It held. She ran faster, darting out from the fence, and then suddenly headed back toward it with a running jump.

"What the . . . !" Dad exclaimed.

Again, she didn't clear the fence. One hind foot caught the barbed wire, tripping her to her knees when she landed on the other side. She struggled to her feet and ran with a limp toward the other cows. They all turned and ran in the other direction with her.

"That . . . heifer! Why did she have to do that?" Dad was angry. "Now there's another section of fence to mend!"

He drove to the gate he had opened for nothing and closed it. Then he drove in silence back to the first gate and along the side of the fence toward home.

Dad stopped to inspect the fence break where the heifer first jumped.

Please don't ask me how this happened, I pleaded silently.

Blackie came running from the yard to greet us. I got out to pet him.

"What happened?" Dad asked from the other side of the pickup. "Why'd she jump?"

I pretended that I hadn't heard, but Dad would not be ignored.

"How'd this happen?" he asked again.

I didn't answer.

"Rachel?"

My hand stopped stroking Blackie's head.

"Rachel?" he called louder. "Do you know what happened?"

I walked to the front of the pickup. Blackie followed.

"Do you know, Rachel, what happened?"

He knew I did.

"Blackie chased her."

"Blackie chased her?"

I nodded my head.

"He's not supposed to be in the cattle yard! Why was he?" He was becoming angry.

I didn't answer, kept my head down.

"That's it! He's going to have to be chained up now!"

The picture of Blackie on the end of a chain, not running around the farm, was dreadful.

"No, Dad!" I protested. "Don't chain him up! I *told* him to sic the cow!"

He looked me in the eyes. "*You* told him . . . to sic the cow?"

I nodded, my hand on Blackie's head.

Dad paused, deciding, then declared, "*You* make sure he doesn't chase a cow again!" He climbed into the pickup and added through the window, "I really don't like having to fix a broken fence that needn't have been broken."

15

Mom! Dad was going to chain Blackie!"

I followed Mom down the clothesline as she wiped the wire clean before hanging the wash on it. At the end of the line she stopped.

"Your dad told me what happened when he came in. He was upset that Blackie chased the heifer and made her jump the fence."

Mom wiped the second wire clean and I walked along. "Did he tell you that I told Blackie to chase her?"

"He mentioned it."

"Did he say that I didn't tell him right away?"

"He did."

"Do you think I'm bad?"

"You were scared and you didn't want your dad to be mad at you."

"That's the last time I'll ever sic Blackie on a cow," I said.

"Never say 'never,'" Mom said. "You may need Blackie's help in a different situation."

"Where's Dad now?"

"He had to meet some cattle buyers at the livestock sale barn."

"What's wrong with him, Mom? He's acting different, scary. He came home drunk. He was really mad about Blackie."

"Your father is hurting deep inside, Rachel. It's affecting everything he does." She hung the clothespin bag on the wire.

"What's causing the hurt? I want it to go away."

Mom lifted a diaper from the wash basket, shook it straight, and pinned one end with a clothespin. It hung limp, waiting.

"Your dad is worried about the soul of our very first baby, born in Iowa." She looked sad. "A baby boy who died of the flu when he was one month old."

"I didn't know we had a baby before Carol."

"We don't talk about it because it's a sad memory." Her voice cracked.

She shook another diaper straight, stretched the first one out, and overlapped the corners, pinning them together with one clothespin.

"It was a terrible time. The worst winter we've lived through. The baby became very ill during a severe snowstorm. The snow was so deep we couldn't drive the car to the doctor in town, so Dad and a neighbor, Henry, hitched the horses to the car. Henry sat on the hood, driving the horses, and your dad was driving the car, hoping to make it easier for the horses. I was in the front seat, too, with the baby in my arms." She paused. "Our baby died on the way to town."

Tears filled her eyes. One tear escaped, and she wiped it from her cheek.

"That's sad, Mom. I'm sorry for you."

She nodded her head and smiled her appreciation.

I took the next diaper and shook it for Mom. She pinned it with the corner of the last one.

"Why does that still bother Dad so much? You're not that way."

"Roger Gene died before he was baptized. Because of that, the minister of our church would not give him a Christian burial. He adhered strictly to the Lutheran belief that 'He who believeth and is baptized shall be saved.' And you know your dad—he's a strict Lutheran."

"He believes the baby isn't saved?" The horror of the possibility stunned me. A picture of a baby burning in hell flashed through my mind. I quickly shut it out. "What do you believe, Mom?"

"I was a Methodist before I married your dad. I

think allowances can be made in some of these church issues."

"Do you think the baby's in heaven?"

"I'm sure of it."

Those were the words I needed to hear.

"Couldn't you convince Dad?"

"He wants to believe it. Part of him does, but he's not absolutely sure. He thinks the Lutheran church and its ministers are God's spiritual leaders to us and what they say is gospel."

I helped Mom hang the rest of the diapers. We didn't speak. When she went to get another basket of wash, I stayed at the line, thinking about what I had just heard, wondering about my first brother.

Mom continued the sad story when she returned. "We had every intention of baptizing our baby. I already had his christening gown." She was reliving the arguments, disbelieving the minister's decision, again.

"The weather was so bad, it was hard to get to church."

"What happened to him? Where's he buried?" I asked.

"He's buried in that Iowa cemetery. All alone."

What a sad, lonely thing for that little baby, I thought.

Mom fingered the kitchen towel she was about to pin to the line. "It was a terrible time," she said again, shaking her head. "Snowstorms raged every day. Your father and I were weak from grief.

"The undertaker had a fine little steel casket with a cross on the top that we bought for Roger. He was buried in his christening gown. We had to drive to the cemetery in a horse-drawn sleigh, cutting fences across fields to get there. How cold that January wind was!

"The undertaker came from town in his horse-drawn hearse. The small grave had been dug and was full of drifted snow. The undertaker gave a short eulogy. Tears filled the eyes of the few women relatives there. Some of the men, too.

"But your dad, he shed no tears. He barely whispered the words of the Lord's Prayer spoken at the end. I think he was afraid his voice would crack and he'd break down.

"After the prayer, the undertaker removed the snow and lowered the casket.

"Those were terrible times," she said again. "Some days I saw that your dad was merely going through the motions of his work. He was so downtrodden about his baby son, worried about his eternal soul. And he blamed himself."

"Why? It wasn't his fault, was it?"

"The snowstorm was already under way when I knew our baby was sick. Your dad was helping our neighbor Henry with a couple of cows that were having trouble birthing their calves. When he got home and I told him that Roger was sick, he thought we should wait a while before heading for the doctor—it looked like the storm might let up. Instead, it got worse. He blamed himself because we waited. For a long time afterward, I'd hear him say, 'If only I hadn't waited . . . ' "

"Poor Dad," I said, shaking my head in sympathy.

"Then the opportunity to buy our own farm in South Dakota came, and I encouraged your dad to buy it. That forced him to think about something else. Soon after that, we knew a new baby would be added to the family. We were a little apprehensive, but when your big sister Carol came into our lives, we were focusing on her and the new farm. Eighteen months later, Kim was born, and then you a couple of years after that. Our focus became you girls and the farm. That piece of doubt Dad had about Roger's soul was pushed to the back of his mind."

"Now I know why Dad looks sad around Matthew," I said.

"Yes. Matthew reminds him of our first son, and I think his hurt, his fear for Roger Gene has come to the surface again." Mom leaned down to get a piece of clothing. It was a flannel pajama top. She shook it and pinned it to the line.

She scooted the wash basket—a recycled apple

bushel basket with a plastic liner and wire handles—farther down the line with her foot.

"Do Carol and Kim know about Roger Gene? That it's affecting Dad again?"

"No. There hasn't been a good time to tell everyone.

"I don't know how Susie would handle this," Mom added. "She's so young and impressionable. She takes everything to heart. I think this could really bother her. You see how she smothers Matthew with her affection. She could become overly worried and too protective toward him."

When Mom finished hanging the basket of wash, I followed her to the back door of the breezeway and down the stairs to the utility room. I wanted to be near her, thinking about the things I had just heard.

She unplugged the washing machine cord from an extension cord. The machine stopped agitating and she removed the round lid. Like thick noodles, the wet clothes dripped with soapy water on her wooden paddle. Each piece that she fed into the wringer emerged flat and stiff on the other side before dropping into the rinse tub.

Mom worked the clothes around a bit in the rinse water with her paddle, then let them sit for a while. She turned the wringer over the empty wash basket and again fed the clothes into the wringer. The plastic liner crackled when the first clothes hit the bottom of the basket.

One of Dad's dress socks stuck to the top wringer roller and wrapped itself around the roller while Mom was fishing another piece from the tub.

"Mom!" I warned, pointing, waking from thoughts of Dad and our first baby.

"Shoot!" she exclaimed, quickly reversing the rollers and unwrapping the sock. At least she caught it before it jammed. I watched Mom fish the last piece from the rinse tub.

"Mom, when is Matthew going to be baptized?"

"Two weeks from tomorrow."

"That seems like a long time. What if something happens to him before then?"

"Nothing is going to happen to him. Besides, I believe God is gracious."

If Matthew should die before he's baptized, I pray thee Lord his soul to take.

One heap of wash remained on the floor near the furnace. Dad's bib overalls, work shirts, dark pants, dark socks, and dark towels would make two more wash loads for Mom.

Mom paused before lifting the filled wash basket. "Rachel, I'd like to tell Carol and Kim about our first baby after I finish the wash. Would you do something with Susie to get her out of the house?"

"Sure, Mom. Susie loves the bridge. I'll take her to the bridge."

16

Susie often asked me to walk to the bridge with her. Mom doesn't let her go by herself yet. It's a ten-minute walk on the gravel road from our place.

I liked going to the bridge, too, but today was different. I was sad about my first baby brother. And Dad. And Mom. And a little anxious about Matthew.

Susie chattered and skipped down the lane to the gravel road. "I'm glad I'm old enough to go to the bridge," she said.

The breeze created a gentle flapping of the wash on the line. The drying shirts ballooned in the wind, swinging upside down from the waist, their arms reaching for the ground. The clothes would be dry soon. Not a cloud threatened the sun.

"It's going to be a long time until Matthew can go to the bridge."

"Mm-hmm," I said. I wasn't much in the mood for talking or listening.

"It's going to be a long time before he can go to school, too," she added.

"Yep."

"Look! There's a frog! He just hopped into the grass." Susie dashed after it, trying to catch it.

"Don't touch it or you'll get warts!" I warned.

"I don't want warts!" She quit her pursuit and walked beside me.

I spotted a garter snake crossing the road a ways ahead of us. Susie is afraid of snakes. Runs screaming into the house to Mom when she sees one.

Cross the road before Susie sees you, snake! Mom is telling Carol and Kim about baby Roger. Wiggle faster!

I slowed my pace, looking ahead to the bridge, hoping Susie would look there, too. The bridge was a sturdy one, just sides, no top or cover. The iron sides started at the road edge, went up at a diagonal, then straight across, higher than the cars and pickups, then down at a diagonal to the road edge on the other side of the creek.

"What are you looking at?" Susie asked.

"The bridge."

"Why?"

"Because."

I saw the tail end of the snake disappear in the grass. *Good!*

When we reached the bridge, our footsteps on the

thick wooden planks echoed in the space between the bridge and the water, scaring the red-winged blackbirds from their perches in the Russian olive bushes along the banks.

We peered down into the water. “How come we can’t see through the water here?” Susie asked. The water was never clear by the bridge.

“Maybe it has something to do with the way the creek snakes back and forth in this area. The water makes a lot of turns and might carry some mud from the banks along with it,” I said.

A turtle was warming itself on the bank.

“See the turtle, Susie!” I pointed. When the turtle heard my voice, it scuttled from its muddy resting place and disappeared into the murky water.

We leaned over the railing and watched the slow September flow of water pass under the bridge. After watching the wavy ripples for a few seconds, I felt like I was moving in the opposite direction of the water.

I picked up a handful of large gravel rocks and went back to the center of the bridge. I gave some to Susie and we took turns dropping them in the water. The ripples moving out in ever-larger circles fascinated Susie. They were fun to watch. Then we dropped rocks together and watched the circles roll over each other.

The sound of a car engine distracted us. We turned

to see our neighbors Otto and Jesse Harmon approaching in their black 1930s coupe. They didn't turn the corner to the bridge, but took the approach into our grassy field and drove near the creek bank.

"Hello, girls!" Jesse called in her high, cheerful voice. "We thought we'd like some fish for supper." She smoothed back a wisp of white hair that had escaped the bun at the back of her head.

"We can't see any fish, Jesse," Susie called to her. "Maybe you'll have to eat something else for supper."

"Oh, don't say that to us!" Otto laughed. He set two five-gallon pails upside down near the edge of the bank for them to sit on. Then he went down to the bank to put water in a pail for the fish they might catch.

I doubted that they would catch anything. Maybe the turtle.

Both of them put a worm on their hooks and dropped the lines into the water. They sat quietly, holding the bamboo poles in their hands, waiting.

"Why aren't they talking?" Susie whispered.

"They don't want to scare the fish," I whispered back.

"Fish just like water noise, huh?"

"I guess."

"We can't drop rocks anymore, can we?"

"Nope." Even our whispers seemed loud.

We stood watching in silence, leaning against the rail. A gentle lapping of the water slowly moving against itself made me sleepy in the midday sun. The red-winged blackbirds braved a return to the Russian olive trees, singing their cheerful songs. On a fence post on the other side of the road, a meadowlark with a bold black handkerchief on its bright yellow breast sang clear, glad notes.

The calm scene was broken by the startling splash of a fish leaping out of the water.

"There's a fish, Jesse!" Susie blurted out.

A swift touch on her arm reminded her to keep still. We waited, hoping the fish would bite on one of their lines.

Where is that fish? It must be getting close to their lines, I thought. I held my breath. Enough time had passed. *It's not going to bite.* I was disappointed for all of us.

Then I saw Jesse respond to the gentle tug on her line. Up came a fish on her hook. She straightened the pole, drew the line toward her, and removed the hook from the fish's mouth. After turning it over and admiring it, she placed it in the pail of water. She raised her arm in a happy wave to us.

"If they don't catch another fish, will one be enough for their dinner?" Susie whispered.

"Sure. Old people don't eat very much," I whispered. I'd heard that somewhere.

The calm was interrupted by the sound of another engine on the road from the other direction. It was Dad's pickup coming around the bend.

Oh, dear! He was back earlier than I had thought he would be. *I wonder how he is. I hope he's not still mad at Blackie and me.*

The planks rumbled when the pickup crossed the bridge. Dad rolled down his window. "Any luck?" he called to Jesse and Otto.

"Caught one big bullhead so far," Otto called back.

"Dad, you're supposed to be quiet so you don't scare the fish," Susie scolded.

"Want a ride home?" he whispered.

"Let's ride!" Susie urged, whispering.

"All right."

"Wait, Tony!" Jesse called. "I have a bag of apples from our orchard for Leona. They make great pie!"

"Much obliged," Dad said. "Rachel, run and get the apples from Jesse."

I ran down the steep ditch, through tall thistly weeds and grass, and up the other side to meet Jesse.

"There you are," Jesse said, handing the big brown paper bag to me.

"Thank you, Jesse," I said. "Good luck with your fishing!"

When I climbed out of the ditch, my jeans were full of scratchy burrs from the weeds. I removed most of them before I climbed into the pickup. Dad seemed okay. We were quiet. Even Susie.

I thought of Carol and Kim and wondered how they took the news of our first brother.

17

Sunday was a quiet, sober day. No one talked much. Except for Susie, we all knew what was bothering Dad.

After church and Sunday school, Mom made a delicious roast for dinner with mashed potatoes and gravy and some sweet corn that she had frozen. I think she was trying to make Dad feel better.

It made us all feel better for a little while. We complimented Mom on the good food. She even found time to make a pie from the apples Jesse had given us. I was looking forward to dessert. I knew we were going to have pie à la mode because I saw the vanilla ice cream in the large deep freezer downstairs.

Except for feeding the cattle, which had to be done every day, we didn't have to work on most Sundays. After dinner, Dad took a nap in his rocker. Matthew took a nap in his crib. Mom was looking through a copy of *Good Housekeeping*. Carol and Kim were in their room. I could hear their radio playing the snappy tune "Hernando's Hideaway." Susie and I were lying on the bed reading, and that song distracted me. When "Hey There, You with the Stars in Your Eyes" started, it was easier to concentrate.

"What's this word, Rachel?" Susie asked. She was reading sentences from a mimeographed paper with large purple-blue letters that Mrs. Bell had sent home for the first graders to practice.

"Play," I told her. "Dick and Jane like to play." I read the whole sentence to her. She repeated the sentence slowly.

"I like to read," Susie said. "Reading is fun." She sounded like the Dick and Jane books.

"I know you do. I like to, too. Now let me."

"All right."

"And don't read out loud."

Susie read a few more sentences, each word by word, then fell asleep.

I was reading a book I found on the bookshelf library in my classroom. Of the dozen or so old books there, *Toby Tyler; or, Ten Weeks with a Circus* appealed most. Toby had decided to run away and join a circus that came through town. He was confessing a few guilt pangs about leaving his stern uncle Daniel, when he realized that his circus master was a cruel man.

The next thing I remember was Dad's voice. "I'm

going to check on the broken fence, Kid, and see if I have everything to fix it."

"Okay, Kid. Are you going to take one of the girls with you?"

"No, I'm just going to look at it."

After I heard the pickup motor, I got up to look out the window. I could see the fence from there. Dad pulled the ends of the barbed wire together. I wondered if he was thinking about his first baby.

The barbed wire wouldn't be hard to fix. I'd seen him do it before. He would attach a stretcher to the broken ends, pull them taut, and join them with a patch of wire wrapped many times around each end. He drove to the broken fence to the east, but that was too far to see from the window.

My arithmetic book on the dresser caught my eye. It was a good time to practice my new method again. Before Susie woke.

And it took my mind off my worries about Dad.

18

Monday morning, I was excited about school. Tuesday would be the next multiplication timed test and I was anxious to try my plan.

"Tomorrow will be the next chance to improve the time and score of your multiplication facts grade and the arithmetic grade on your report card," Mrs. Kelly reminded us.

I had taken my book home and practiced my method several times. I took my arithmetic book home again Monday night for one last practice.

When the bus drove into our lane, I noticed that the garage door was open and the car was gone.

I was first in the kitchen door. "Mom, where's Dad?" I asked. Carol and Kim were right behind me.

Mom glanced out the window at Susie, who was playing with a barn kitten. "Your dad felt a sudden need to visit Roger Gene's grave in Iowa. I thought it might be good for him and encouraged him to go."

Just then, Susie came in the kitchen door. She was carrying the kitten that was out front when we got off the bus.

"Susie! You know you can't bring the kitten in the house," I scolded her.

"Rachel's right! Out with the kitten, Susie!" Mom said.

"Where's Dad?" she asked, ignoring the orders and petting the black-and-white cat in her arms.

"Susie," Mom warned in a last-chance voice.

"All right." Susie backed to the door slowly and left the kitchen. We listened as she walked through the breezeway.

After we heard the outside door open, Mom said softly, "I told him to go. Said we could handle things here."

"Where's Daddy?" Susie asked when she came back. She held only her lunch pail this time.

"He went to Iowa," Mom answered.

"Where's Iowa?" Susie asked.

"It's about two hundred fifty miles southeast of us," Mom said. "That's a five-hour drive out and a five-hour drive back," she added for everyone's benefit. "And, I don't know if he will make it back tonight."

"If we had a telephone, he could call us and let us—"

"Carol!" Mom interrupted. "Not the telephone

gripe today. You know it would cost a lot of money to bring the line two miles to us," Mom pointed out. "We have more important things to deal with right now."

Carol had a point, I thought. We girls pleaded for a phone from time to time, mostly so we could talk to our friends. Dad refused for that very reason, said we'd be talking on it all the time.

Then one of us would argue, "It would be good to have one in an emergency."

His answer was always, "They never work when you need them in an emergency."

"What's Dad doing in Iowa?" Susie asked.

Matthew's waking cry cut the telephone complaints short and distracted Susie.

"Who wants to get Matthew?" Mom asked.

"I'll get him," I volunteered.

"Me, too," Susie said.

"Remember to support his head, Rachel," Mom reminded. "And change his diaper if he's wet."

"Hello, Matthew," Susie cooed to him between the wooden slats of his crib. "We're going to get you out of there. How would you like that?"

He stopped crying. I gently rolled him over on his back. I checked the diaper beneath his rubber pants. "He's wet, but at least he isn't dirty," I said. "It doesn't smell like he has a dirty diaper, anyway."

With one hand under his neck and head and the

other under his body, I lifted Matthew from his crib and laid him on the flannel-covered rubber pad on Mom's bed. I pulled the rubber pants off his little legs and asked Susie to get me a clean diaper. She took the top one from the pile of folded white cloth diapers on Mom's dresser.

"Why does he pee so much?" Susie asked when she saw his wet diaper.

"Well, look at his tiny body! Where is all that milk going to stay?" I didn't really know the answer, but that made sense to me.

I undid the safety pins. With one hand, I put Matthew's little feet together and lifted his legs and bottom to remove the wet diaper the way Mom did. When I placed the diaper in the covered diaper pail, a faint smell of ammonia escaped.

I placed the clean diaper under him. Mom had the long rectangles folded in half and in half again to make the perfect fit for Matthew's little bottom. Susie held the baby powder and I let her sprinkle a little on him before pinning the diaper. I made sure the safety locks were pressed down on the pins before pulling on his rubber pants.

"I bet that feels better, huh, Matthew?" I picked him up carefully with one hand under his neck and settled him in the crook of my arm.

Through Mom's open window came the call of a male pheasant. "Hear that pheasant, Matthew?

That's our state bird. Someday you'll have to know that for school."

He fixed his gaze on me. "Yes, it's our state bird," I repeated.

"Why do you talk to him like that?" Susie asked.

"Because he listens and he likes it," I answered.

"Does he understand what you're saying?"

"Probably not, but look how he listens!" I turned so she could see him better. "The *coyote* is the state animal. The *walleye* is the state fish," I said slowly with emphasis, smiling, too. He kicked his little legs and looked into my eyes.

"Let's head for the kitchen, Matthew, and see what the family's doing. Well, all except Dad." I almost added, "Your daddy is heartbroken," but caught myself in time, since Mom didn't think Susie should worry.

"Here's Matthew, Mom!" Susie announced. "We changed his diaper."

"We?" I asked.

"Well, I helped," she said.

"Thanks, girls." Mom was slicing the leftover roast beef for sandwiches. A loaf of soft white, evenly sliced Old Home bread lay open on the counter. It was the kind of bread you could roll into a ball between your hands, pop into your mouth for one big bite.

A small bottle of baby formula was heating in a

saucepan of water on the stove. Another large pan contained several bottles being sanitized in boiling water. And the water used for Matthew's formula had to be boiled first, too.

"If this is ready you can feed him, Rachel, while I make these sandwiches." Mom held up her wrist and let a couple of drops of formula drip on the tender side. "That's warm enough," she said. She pulled out a chair from the table for me and when I was settled, handed me the bottle. "There you go. I should have the sandwiches ready when Carol and Kim finish feeding the cattle."

I heard Mom's brisk movements at the kitchen counter. It was a contrast to the rhythmic sucking of Matthew, who didn't know about our first brother and Dad's sadness.

Susie was biting her fingernails and looking out the window toward the mile corner.

"What are you looking at?" I asked.

"I'm watching for Dad," she said.

Mom heard. "Honey, it's way too soon for your dad to come home. That will be long after you've gone to bed."

"Why did he go to Iowa, Mom?"

Mom hesitated. I knew she was looking for the right time to tell Susie about Roger Gene. I guess she didn't feel up to it then because she said, "He had some important business to take care of, Susie." Her matter-of-fact tone made that the answer to the question for tonight.

The evening was long. Carol was getting her high school initiation costume together. The freshman girls had to dress in bib overalls like men, and the boys had to dress like women. Carol brought a bucket from the barn. She was to bring it with cleaning items. Mom helped her gather those. She gave her a half-full bottle of Pine-Sol, a can of Ajax cleanser, a scrub brush, and an old dishtowel for a dust cloth.

Susie was playing the only record she had. I think it was given to us when we bought the new cabinet radio with a record player inside. "Whistle While You Work" and "Peter Cottontail" would have lifted my spirits on another day; but I, like everyone else, was worried about Dad.

I sat at the kitchen table with my arithmetic book and practiced for the timed test. I was using the backs of old business letters Dad had given me. He thought using new paper for practice was wasteful. It was hard to concentrate. I started and stopped a lot. Asked Susie to turn down the record player. On one try without stops, my time was one minute and twenty-five seconds. *I hope I can do that tomorrow,* I thought.

It was strange not to hear the sound of Dad's voice that night. Mom went to bed alone. Dad's absence was felt in every room of the house.

Susie and I knelt together by our bed for our nighttime prayer. "Now I lay me down to sleep; I pray thee Lord my soul to keep. If I should die before I wake, I pray thee Lord my soul to take."

I started to get up but waited when Susie added, "Dear God, please help Daddy make it home tonight."

19

Susie's prayer was not answered.

Matthew's crying woke me the next morning. Susie, too. Then we heard Mom at Carol and Kim's door. "Carol, Kim, you'll have to feed the cattle before breakfast. Your dad didn't make it home last night." They groaned, put on their work clothes, and were quickly out the door.

Susie and I went to the kitchen. Mom was holding Matthew. I think she had been crying, because her eyes were red.

Mom tried to soothe Matthew. She fed him a bottle, but he only took a few swallows and then started crying again. She jiggled him on her shoulder but that didn't help. Susie tried to comfort him. That didn't help.

"Girls, will you set the table? We're having cold cereal this morning." Susie and I had it ready and had time to get dressed before Carol and Kim returned.

"I've decided to drive over to Hall's after the bus comes and call Aunt Lily from there.

"If we had a phone—"

"Well, we don't!" Mom cut Kim off. Matthew started fussing again.

Carol and Kim left to get dressed for school. Susie and I cleared the table.

When the bus came, Carol was a sight. "You look funny, Carol," Susie said. She had on a pair of Dad's bib overalls with the pant legs rolled up, one of his farmer caps with a frayed bill, and a pair of his old work shoes. Her books were in one arm and the pail of cleaning materials in the other. "Might as well forget about dignity today," she said. She tossed her head to swing the hair out of her work collar.

"Lipstick!" she exclaimed when she was at the kitchen door. "I forgot my lipstick! We were told that we must have a tube of lipstick!" She put down her books and pail and rushed back to her room. She returned with a tube in her hand.

"Mom, I hope you get good news about Dad today," Carol said before she walked out.

"Maybe he'll be home when we get home," Kim said.

"I hope so," Mom said.

Susie gave her a hug. "Bye, Mom." She patted Matthew's bottom, the part she could reach, since he was quiet for a while over Mom's shoulder. "Bye, Matthew. You be good for Mom today. Please."

I hesitated before saying goodbye. A part of me wanted to stay home and keep Mom company, but the other part wanted to show off my speed in arithmetic class today.

"Goodbye, Mom," I finally said.

"Goodbye, dear."

I got to the bus in time to hear Les say, "Good morning, *Mr.* Carol!"

There was a commotion when Carol climbed on the bus. "Look at her!" someone exclaimed. Her bucket clanged against the seats. When she reached her seat with Mona, she sat down, exasperated.

One of the senior boys sitting in the back of the bus moved up beside her. "Did you bring your lipstick?" he asked.

"Yes," she answered meekly.

"Give it to me." She did. "You know, you don't have near enough lipstick on today," he teased. Then he drew wide red lines around her lips.

She looked goofy. She didn't dare disobey or refuse directions because then the seniors would target her and give punishments.

"All right, that's enough now, Dean!" Les said, looking in his rear-view mirror. "Back to your own seat."

The excitement of Carol's initiation calmed down after the bus turned the corner. The bridge planks rumbled, Les shifted to high gear, and we were on our way to the next stop.

When we arrived at school, a crowd was gathered around the freshmen, watching the seniors make them do ridiculous things.

Carol and her friend Jan had to scrub bird poo off the sidewalk. Carol's Pine-Sol and brush came in handy.

One of the boys in a dress, high heels, and a hairnet had to push the merry-go-round full of kids. The high heels made him stumble a lot, and everyone laughed at him.

Seniors made freshmen carry their books for them all day. Freshmen had to follow seniors to their classes, put the books on their desks, and then rush to their own classes.

During recess, a few of us watched through the glass doors of the high school assembly hall. Students were passing to classes and I saw Carol with her arms full of books, following a senior girl with no books. All the freshmen had lipstick-painted faces, in various degrees, depending on the mercy of their superiors.

"Outside, girls!" Mrs. Kelly reminded us. We hadn't heard her coming.

I felt nervous during recess because our multiplication test was right afterward. I had my heart set on being fastest and best.

After recess, I took a short drink at the fountain outside our classroom door because I wanted to get ready for the test. Others took their usual long drinks. "Two more minutes," Mrs. Kelly warned the remaining students. *I think she knows that sometimes our long drinks are a ploy to get out of a few minutes of class,* I thought.

I slid into my seat, took out my arithmetic book, and removed a piece of notebook paper, accidentally letting the ring clasps shut with a loud click. Embarrassed, I started the heading on my paper, feigning innocence. In the right-hand corner I wrote "Arithmetic" on the first line, "Rachel Johnson" on the second line, and "September 28, 1954" on the third line, the way Mrs. Kelly wanted us to. I did that carefully.

We kept our arithmetic books closed, with our papers marking the page of the facts. When Mrs. Kelly said, "Begin," books flopped open, papers were folded, and pencils started scratching on paper.

My pencil dashed across the page. I was the first one to fold my paper. My special plan was working. I had memorized the answers across each row, so all I had to do was write the answers. I wrote as fast as I could but was careful to form the numbers correctly.

When done, I whipped my book shut and let out a loud sigh—as much to let everyone know that I was done as to release tension.

I shot my hand into the air for Mrs. Kelly to see. She had heard me and put her finger to her lips to signal quiet, but her eyes showed amazement. She wrote "1:20" on the board. My best time yet!

I felt eyes on me. Fifth graders for only a second, but sixth graders were watching, too.

The next best time on the board was "1:35" for Melissa and then "1:38" for Darren.

I exchanged papers with Melissa. I listened for her pencil as Mrs. Kelly read each answer. It didn't mark any wrong.

Melissa had a perfect paper. One of her zeros looked a little like a six, but I let it go. When she returned my paper, an A+ was at the top in her perfect handwriting.

I did it! I had the best time! I had the best score!

The sixth graders were watching, too, when Mrs. Kelly said, "Well done, Rachel!"

—

I was hoping that things at home would be as good as they had been in school. But they weren't. Dad was not home when the bus dropped us off.

I was the first one in the door. Susie was right behind me. “Mom, what’d you find out about Dad?” I asked.

Mom sighed. “He stayed at Lily’s last night. He wanted another day . . . for his business. He plans on being home later tonight.”

20

"Where is Daddy eating supper, Mom?" Susie asked while we were eating our supper of pancakes and bacon.

"Maybe at Aunt Lily's. Maybe a café somewhere."

At eight o'clock, Dad still was not home. I was at the kitchen table trying to beat today's time on the multiplication test. I was writing the answers on the page margins of *Farm Journal* magazines. I had run out of old letters with blank backs.

Susie was in the living room reading to Mom. And Matthew.

At 8:30, Mom made Susie go to bed. "Let me kiss Matthew, Mom." I imagined her pecking the plump cheek of her baby brother sleeping on his mother's shoulder. When Susie went to her room, Mom got up from her rocking chair and laid Matthew in his crib.

"Mom?" Susie called from the bedroom when she heard Mom come out of hers.

Mom walked to her room. "Yes, Susie?"

I could barely hear Susie, but she asked, "Do you think Daddy's coming home tonight?"

"I do," Mom said, "but it'll be later."

"Good."

"Did you remember your prayer?" Mom asked.

Then I heard, faintly, Susie's voice in rhythmic tones as Mom listened to her bedtime prayer. I strained to hear if she added, "Please, dear God, let Daddy come home." She did.

Please, dear God, let Dad come home, I prayed, too. *And help him not to be sad,* I added.

Mom came to the kitchen to check on me. "How are you doing, dear?"

"Pretty good.

"Mom?"

"Yes, dear?"

"What did Dad say on the phone?"

"He wanted another day to think and visit Roger's grave. I told him we understood," she said softly. "He'll be home tonight. I'm quite sure of it.

"Working on that timed test again?" she asked when she saw my math book.

"I want to see if I can beat today's time. I got one minute and twenty seconds. Best in the class. No mistakes."

"Good for you." She headed toward the kitchen door.

"Where are you going?" I asked.

"I'm going down to the fruit cellar to see if we have any canned peaches left. I thought peaches would taste good for breakfast."

Every fall Dad bought a couple crates of Oregon peaches. They were large and juicy, smelled good, and were so pretty in the crates—each rose-tinged yellow-orange peach wrapped in its own decorated tissue paper. Mom canned some of them. But not this year. Dad hadn't bought any.

Mom left the kitchen door open. I listened to her soft-soled steps down the stairs, through the basement hall, and into the far back room where it was cool. The fruit cellar was directly below Mom and Dad's bedroom. *And Matthew's.*

I went to check on him, slowly opening the door, hoping it wouldn't squeak and wake him. He lay on his tummy, his curled fists by the sides of his head. The light from the hall was too dim to see if he was breathing. Gently, I laid my hand on his back. The steady rising and falling reassured me. I kept my hand there because it didn't seem to bother him. I whispered, "Next Sunday, Matthew, your home in heaven will be clinched."

"What are you doing?" Mom's whisper from the door startled me.

"I . . . I wanted to make sure Matthew was all right," I whispered back.

"Rachel, don't worry. He's fine." She coaxed me out of the room.

"What about Dad?" I asked.

"I'm sure he'll be home soon."

I had no reply. I wished I could say, "Don't worry, Mom, he's fine," but I couldn't.

"I'm going to bed now, Mom. Good night."

"Good night, Rachel."

I wanted to read, so I switched the light on, hoping I wouldn't wake Susie.

I sympathized with Toby Tyler, whose circus master made him work hard and beat him. The last thing I remembered was the monkeys, including Toby's special monkey friend, escaping from their circus cage before hushed voices in the kitchen woke me.

"Oh, Kid, I'm so glad you're home. The girls are worried. I was worried. Are you hungry?" Mom said.

"A few graham crackers and milk will do," Dad answered. "I had an early supper at Lily's before I started."

I fell asleep to the sounds of Mom getting crackers and milk for Dad.

21

The next morning, Dad was feeding the cattle at breakfast time.

Carol and Kim asked Mom about Dad's trip.

"He's thinking about things," she replied, not willing to relate particulars.

"What's taking him so long this morning?" Kim asked.

"He got a late start."

No one spoke for a while. We heard each other crunching cold cereal.

Susie broke the near silence. "My prayer was answered, Mom."

"Yes, it was." Mom nodded.

"What was your prayer?" Carol asked.

"That Daddy come home."

Carol nodded too, like Mom.

"Matthew's sleeping late this morning," I said. I gave Mom a questioning look.

"He was up early and I gave him a bottle. Then he seemed sleepy, so I put him back down." She smiled knowingly. "He's fine, Rachel."

Dad still wasn't in from chores when we boarded the bus. I caught a glimpse of him in the cattle yard down the hill. He was checking the water level of the circular wooden stock tank. In this September warm spell, the slow-flowing artesian well had a hard time supplying enough water for the thirsty cattle.

The bus was quieter this morning. I knew why my sisters and I were quiet, but not the others. Even the rambunctious high school boys were behaving themselves.

When we picked up the Rockford sisters, our last stop, time was getting close for the achievement tests. I wanted to do well this year, first in the class, I hoped.

After the bell rang, Mrs. Kelly said, "Make sure you have two sharpened pencils for the tests." A line of fifth graders rushed to the pencil sharpener on the doorjamb and a line of sixth graders to the sharpener on the window ledge.

The achievement tests began right after the pledge. Mrs. Kelly handed out the test booklets, instructing us to leave them closed until she told us to open them. When everyone had a booklet she read from her manual, "On these tests, you are not expected to know the answers to all of the questions. Answer as many as you can. For those of which you are not sure, mark the answer you think is best. Your wrong answers will not be counted against you. If you finish before time is called, you may go back and check your work, but only on that test. You may not turn back to any other tests."

The spelling test was first. Mrs. Kelly gave directions to the sixth grade and the fifth graders listened. Then we had an assignment in our history book.

When it was time for the fifth-grade test, we opened our booklets to a page of twenty-four words, each spelled four different ways. We had to choose the correct spelling and fill in the circle in front of our choice.

Mrs. Kelly read the word, used it in a sentence, and read it again. Then we marked our choice. At number 14, Mrs. Kelly said, "Family. There are four children in the family. Family."

There are five children in our family. Once there was one more. I wonder how Matthew is doing?

O famly
O famaly
O family
O familie

I penciled in the third choice.

During Mrs. Kelly's pause, my mind wandered to Mom, Dad, and Matthew. *What's Matthew doing now?* I glanced up at the clock. *A little past nine? Is Mom holding him? Burping him? Is he crying?*

"Sham-ee," Mrs. Kelly said. She didn't give the sentence and students' heads were down.

I missed the sentence! Sham-ee? I've never heard the word before! I looked at the choices:

O shamme
O chamois
O shamee
O chammie

I marked the third one.

The words got harder. I did a lot of guessing. The last word Mrs. Kelly said was, "Muh-nu-ver. His last-minute muh-nu-ver made it possible for him to win the race. Muh-nu-ver."

I'd heard the word before and understood the sentence, but I had never seen or read the word.

I studied the choices:

O manuver
O maneuver
O menuever
O manuever

and marked the first one.

When the spelling test was finished, Mrs. Kelly said, "Put your pencils down and close your tests.

Just relax for a minute before we begin the grammar test."

Everyone was quiet. Mrs. Kelly looked at a couple of pages in her test manual. Then she said, "The directions for the grammar test are the same for both grades, but the tests are different, with different times. Sixth graders, you will have twenty-five minutes, fifth graders, twenty minutes."

After Mrs. Kelly had read the directions aloud and we had worked the examples, she said, "Begin!" with a pronounced nod of her head that reminded me of the flag signal at the start of the stock car races I'd seen at the state fair last year.

The first questions were easy grammar. Number 6 was

> "The old tombstones _was / were_ cracked."

I circled "were."

What kind of tombstone does Roger Gene have? Is it cracked? Is it carved?

It was hard to concentrate on the questions after that one. I marked the last one as Mrs. Kelly said, "Stop! Time is up!"

Recess was a relief. Lance and David appointed themselves captains of Pom Pom Pullaway. Most kids played but a few chose to swing, jump rope, swing on the giant strikes, or climb on the monkey bars.

Half of the Pom Pom Pullaway kids lined up along the side of the school, the other half along the school fence about sixty feet away.

"I'll be It," Lance announced, then called, "Pom Pom Pullaway! Come away or I'll pull you away!" We dashed across, hoping to get to opposite sides before Lance tagged any of us. He tagged Lester. Now they were both It.

Lance called again, "Pom Pom Pullaway! Come away or we'll pull you away!" We dashed across again. Lance tagged Darren and Lester tagged Melissa. I dodged past Melissa in the next "pullaway." I was pretty fast. Last year I won third place in the girls' one-hundred-yard dash at the county track meet. The next pullaway, Lester and Melissa both chased me. I escaped them. I knew they would be after me on the next run. The bell rang, and we walked panting to the front door.

"We'll get you next recess, Rachel!" Melissa vowed, catching up to me. A warm flush colored her smiling face. Lester was behind her.

"Maybe," I said, but I knew I didn't have much of a chance. There were a lot of kids in the It group.

Between the recesses, we had two reading tests. I was able to concentrate on those better than the earlier tests.

We continued Pom Pom Pullaway at noon. I

was the last girl tagged. David was the last boy. We started another round and David was It.

In the afternoon we had two arithmetic tests—computation and story problems. I kept my concentration for computation, which started with easy addition and ended with hard multiplication and hard division problems.

When I finished the problems I knew how to work, I broke the longer ones into steps, multiplied the thousands, hundreds, tens, and ones separately, and then added them together. On some, I even matched one of the choices. I felt I had done the best I could when Mrs. Kelly said, "Time!"

In the story problem test, I was reading, "Mr. Jones drove a total of 80 miles to and from work during each five-day workweek. How far did he live from work?" and thought, *Dad drove five hundred miles to visit Roger's grave. I hope it helped him not to worry about him.*

The scratching of Melissa's pencil on paper brought my attention back to the test. I still had half the test to do and the problems were getting harder.

I knew I wasn't going to finish and I didn't—didn't even have time to guess at the last few.

I was glad it was the last test for the day.

22

Dad was in his pickup in the west pasture checking the cattle when the bus turned on our mile road.

I knew Carol and Kim were as anxious to find out more about Dad as I was. We wasted no time getting into the house. When Blackie came running around from the shady side of the garage where he liked to lie on warm days, I said, "Hello, Blackie! Goodbye, Blackie!" I gave him a token pat on the head before entering the house.

"Mom?" Carol called when Mom wasn't in the kitchen. Hearing no answer, she walked to the bedroom.

"She's not in the bedroom," Carol said.

"Matthew?" I asked.

"Nope."

"I'll check the basement," I said. "Maybe she's way back in the fruit cellar and can't hear us."

"I don't think she'd take Matthew down there," Kim said.

"Well, where are they?" I demanded of her. "I'm going to check the basement anyway." I ran down the stairs, opened the door to the spare bedroom, then the fruit cellar. No Mom.

"Mom?" I heard Kim call outside from the back breezeway door. Mom wasn't behind the house tending flowers, pumping the septic tank, hanging clothes on the line, burning papers, doing any chores that got done behind the house.

"Where could she be with Matthew?" I asked.

"Is the car here?" Kim asked, and then opened the breezeway door to the garage. The car was there.

"Maybe she's riding with Dad," Susie said.

"With the baby? In that bumpy pasture in the pickup?" I said.

There were no other places to look, so we changed our clothes and waited. When the pickup returned, Mom, with Matthew, got out.

"He really enjoyed the ride," Mom said.

"Over all those bumps?" I asked. The pasture had prairie dog holes, badger holes, rocks hidden in grass, and deep hoof prints from wet weather.

"Your dad drove slow and it wasn't too bad."

"Can I hold him?" I reached my arms out to get him.

"*May* I hold him," Carol quickly corrected me.

Mom handed Matthew to me. I held him over my shoulder. "I know. Hold his head," I said before Mom could remind me. He felt heavier, was bigger. He wore his baby nightgown that closed at the bottom with a pull string.

I held him close to my face, making it easier for me to look at Dad and gauge his feelings. He still seemed sad. His trip to Iowa must not have solved things for him.

—

The next morning, a high layer of clouds covered the whole sky and the air was muggy. The flies had become persistent pests in the humid weather, and a few had found their way into the house. Mom kept a fly swatter handy.

"It feels like it could rain," Dad said when he returned for breakfast after feeding the cattle their ground corn. "We sure could use it. The pastures are brown and the east dugout is almost dry.

"It's about time to sell these fat cattle." He nodded in the direction of the west yard. "They're ready. They drink a lot of water, too, and the well is having a hard time keeping up."

"And we could use the money," he added, speaking more to himself than to anyone else.

There was sadness in his eyes. Matthew's baptism was only three days away. That was important to him, but I was sure that Dad was thinking about his other son, too.

23

It started sprinkling on the way to school. I saw the drops on the bus windshield. I wished I had Mom's fly swatter, because the pesky flies in the bus clung to us in a frenzy.

By the time we got to school, it was pouring. We all made a mad dash from the bus to the school doors.

We had intelligence tests first thing after the pledge. Those were more fun than the academics. Many of the questions seemed like puzzles:

> "Which shape is the same?"

You had to choose the topsy-turvy shape from among a few others all very similar to the shape in the question. Or:

> "What is the next number in this row: 2, 3, 5, 8, __?"

The possible answers given were "10, 11, 12, 13."

It was still pouring at recess time. Out the window, thick dotted lines of water dropped from the dark gray sky.

Recess was indoors and everyone went down to the gym. We had to take our shoes off to protect the shiny wooden floor. I remembered a hole in my sock toe and sank to the lowest bleacher seat in dismay. Several of the kids were playing tag, and I would have to watch all the fun from the bleachers.

"Rachel?" Melissa said. "What's wrong? Don't you feel good?"

"I'm all right." I couldn't tell her about my sock. It was too embarrassing and she might think I was poor.

"Come on, Rachel! I want a chance to tag you!" Lance said. He had volunteered to be It.

I shook my head.

"Come on, chicken!" he goaded. Then he chased after Winnie, tagging her. Winnie tagged Melissa. Melissa chased Lester. He let her tag him. They ran in and out of others playing basketball. Lester ran after David and couldn't catch him. Darren ran near Lance and dodged his shoulder just in time. My shoulder dodged too, on the bleacher.

Maybe no one will notice my toe. Quickly, I untied my shoes, pulled the holey sock long, turned it under my foot, and joined the game. Lance took advantage of my slow start and slapped a rough tag on my back as I tried to run away.

David was the last one tagged and he was It for the next game. I let him tag me right away. *All right, Lance, where are you?* He was my target. I kept a sly eye on him while pretending to chase others. I sensed him sneaking up behind me, did a surprise turn, and slapped a hard tag on his shoulder. "You're It!"

"Ouch!" he cried when I dashed past.

"You're such a baby!" I taunted from a safe distance.

"You're a cooked goose, Rachel Johnson!" he yelled, lunging toward me. I dodged behind the kids playing basketball and used Greg, a sixth grader, as a shield. He guarded me from Lance for a few seconds until a member of his team yelled, "Greg!" and threw the ball to him.

My shield was gone!

"Ring! Ring! Ring! Ring!" *Mrs. Kelly! Thank you!* Mrs. Kelly was in the doorway at the top of the bleachers ringing her brass bell. Lance wouldn't dare touch me.

Kids scrambled to the bleachers, retrieving shoes.

"Raachel," Lance said, a "gotcha" tone in his voice. I looked at him and he pointed to my foot. "You have a hole in your sock!" he said, loud enough for many to hear.

My face got hot. I sensed kids looking at my sock. I shoved that foot into its shoe. I walked quietly up two flights of stairs, avoiding everyone's eyes.

Winnie walked beside me. "Lance is a jerk! No one cares about a hole in a sock." She made me feel a little better.

We had one more test after recess. Then the whole room had the same penmanship lesson. We practiced two lines of connected ovals, two lines of up-and-down strokes for warm-up. Then on a piece of school paper with a shiny smooth finish, we copied the poem "Trees." I held my breath while I copied the last two lines.

Poems are made by fools like me,
But only God can make a tree.

I sighed in relief because I had made it without any inkblots spoiling the paper.

Outside, the sky was a lighter gray and the rain had become steady and gentle. The gray sky made the classroom dark enough to use lights. Six round glass shades in two rows were hanging from the ceiling by narrow pipes. The lights and the gray sky outside gave the classroom a cozy, calm feeling.

Smells from the cafeteria on the first floor drifted up the stairs and under the door. I smelled one of my favorite school foods—chili con carne.

When it was time for lunch, most of the third and fourth graders had already gone through the line. Waiting in line along the cafeteria counter, I saw slices of cheddar cheese, soda crackers, carrot and celery sticks, and brownies. At the end of the line, white or chocolate milk was served in glasses with curves like they used in cafés. I liked seeing the milk through the glass. At home, we drank from colored metal tumblers because they didn't break. We took our meal trays to long tables with benches along the sides. I ate everything on my tray.

For noon recess, I was grateful that we had the choice of playing in the gym or doing quiet games in the classroom. I couldn't endure the embarrassment of my holey sock after morning recess. Melissa, Winnie, Jenny, a sixth-grade friend, and I stayed in the room and played Hangman.

Melissa and I paired off. I was hangman first. I looked at Melissa with a smug smile and said, "I've got a tough one." I drew the hangman's pole and seven blanks with white chalk on the chalkboard.

"A," Melissa said for her first guess.

I wrote *a* on the third blank.

"E."

I shook my head and drew a circle head under the line on the hanging pole. I wrote *e* off to the side where the wrong guesses would go.

"B?"

"Nope!" I drew one side of the neck and wrote *b* to the side.

"I?"

I wrote *i* on the sixth blank.

"Hmmm." Melissa thought briefly. "N?"

I drew the second side of the neck and recorded *n* with the wrong guesses.

"O?"

I wrote *o* in the fifth blank.

"Oy?" Melissa thought aloud when she saw the *oi* together.

"L?"

I shook my head, drew one shoulder, and recorded it.

"P?"

Second shoulder.

"Hooow about C?"

"Yep." I filled in the first blank.

Melissa frowned. Even when she frowned, her dimples formed.

"R?"

Shaking my head, I drew one side of the body.

"Not C-R?" Melissa thought aloud. "C-L?"

I pointed to the list. "You already guessed 'L.'"

"H! C-H!" Melissa rose to her tiptoes in glee.

I wrote *h* in the second blank. *Only two letters left. She could guess this.*

"Char?" she questioned. "No, I guessed 'R' already," she corrected herself. She paused, and I heard the sixth-grade girls playing Cat and Mouse on the side chalkboard.

"T?" Melissa asked after thinking.

I shook my head, smiled, and drew the other side of the body.

"S?"

"Eeww! One letter to go," I said, then wrote *s* on the last line.

"M!"

I wrote *m* in the fourth and last blank and said, "Congratulations!" to Melissa.

"What *is* that word? It was on our spelling test," Melissa said.

"It's 'chamois.' I asked my big sister Carol because I didn't know what it was either. She said it's a soft cloth for cleaning."

I erased the partially hung figure and letters and gave the chalk to Melissa. She thought for a minute before her face lit up with a good idea. She had a lot of hangman lines drawn before I guessed her word—"meadowlark."

"Let's play school," Winnie suggested. Mrs. Kelly had been out of the room for a while. The other kids in the room had left for the gym.

"I'll be teacher," Winnie said. The three of us took front seats.

"Now sit up straight and pay attention!" she said, mimicking authority. We straightened our shoulders and pulled our chins up.

"What are we going to study, teacher?" Melissa asked, assuming an attentive manner.

"You are going to study *Proper Speech!*"

"*Proper Speech!*" I mimicked.

"Rachel! Repeat after me! Peter Piper picked a peck of pickled peppers!"

"Peter Piper picked a peck of pickled peppers!"

"Too slow!" she quipped. "Melissa, let's hear you say it!"

"Peter Piper picked a peck of pickled peppers!" She rattled it faster than I did.

"Very good!"

"Jenny!"

"Do I have to?" Jenny challenged.

"Yes! Unless you want an F in *Proper Speech!*" Winnie's serious demeanor caused the three of us to break out in laughter. Then Jenny mimicked Winnie. "An F in *Proper Speech!*" And we laughed as hard all over again. Eventually we regained our composure, but our lesson in proper speech was over.

"My turn!" I said. Winnie took my seat. I stood in front. "Now, students, it's time for your geography lesson!" I pressed my hand genteelly on my upper chest.

"Where are our books?" Winnie asked.

"Here they are!" I handed each a pretend book. "Open your books to page forty-five!"

They did. Each in her own way. Winnie pretended to gauge where page forty-five was and opened it to the spot. I smiled and nodded approval. Melissa paged through the book, taking her time. "Uh, Melissa. Page forty-five!" I reminded her, my hand in genteel gesture again. "Jenny, did you get a brand-new book?" She was opening the book every few pages and pressing lightly down.

"Are you to page forty-five yet, Jenny?" I feigned impatience.

"Yes, teacher."

"I think you should know by now that my name is . . . Mrs. Smart."

They snickered.

"I'll have none of that!" I pointed a warning finger at them.

"We are studying the continent of Asia, the largest continent in the world!" I had listened to the sixth-grade lessons on Asia last week. "One of the major countries in Asia is India!"

I remembered that one of the new maps rolled up over the chalkboard was of Asia. I went to the board and pulled down that map. "There! The continent of Asia! Who can show me where India is?"

They looked at each other, dumbfounded, shook their heads, and held out their hands palms up to indicate they had no idea.

"Goodness gracious!" I grabbed Mrs. Kelly's yardstick, hanging from its nail on the chalkboard frame, and turned back to the map. "Now, this is where India is!" I swung the end of the yardstick emphatically to India to impress its location forever in their minds.

The sound of paper ripping where the metal tip of the yardstick hit India stunned me. The other three gasped. In the middle of the pink triangular shape representing India was a big rip.

"Holy smoke!" I froze. A sick feeling spread in my stomach.

"Quick! Roll up the map!" Winnie said.

I did. And then replaced the yardstick on its nail.

"Let's play Hangman again," I said. "Pretend like nothing happened." We scurried to the board and started rounds of Hangman, subdued by the guilt of the ripped map.

What will I do next time Mrs. Kelly rolls the map down and finds the rip? I thought.

My stomach was still feeling sick when the bell rang a few minutes later and the kids returned from the gym followed by Mrs. Kelly. I couldn't look at her. I was afraid she would see the guilt on my face.

I paged through my reading text. Melissa and Winnie were acting occupied, too.

When everyone was settled after drinks, Mrs. Kelly sat behind her desk and opened *Call It Courage*. She read to us longer than she usually did.

I was grateful. The problems of Mafatu, the Polynesian boy stranded alone on an island, made me forget my troubles. Mafatu wanted to kill a wild boar with a knife he had made so he could return to his island with the tusks to prove that he was not the Boy Who Was Afraid. But first he was forced to kill a hammerhead shark with his knife to save his dog. He also needed the knife to make a canoe with sails to cross the ocean to his island and escape the eaters-of-men he had discovered. In an accident while fishing from his handmade raft, he lost his knife in deep, deep water.

"To make another knife so fine would take days," Mrs. Kelly read. "Without it he was seriously handicapped. He *must* get his knife! But . . .

"The reef-wall looked dark and forbidding in the fading light. Its black holes were the home of the giant *feké*—the octopus . . ." Mrs. Kelly smiled a devilish smile as she placed the bookmark in the page and closed the book.

We all groaned. She knew she had us hooked for the next "Literature Aloud" session.

The map-ripping incident again pushed its way to the front of my thoughts and the sick feeling returned. I was now the Girl Who Was Afraid. Then Mrs. Kelly announced that we would have our "Weekly Reader" before recess because after recess Mrs. Ohlman, the third- and fourth-grade teacher, had invited us to join her classes for square-dancing in the gym.

This wasn't my day. We would have to square-dance, which I liked, but—we also would have to take off our shoes.

When I opened my "Weekly Reader," my stomach plummeted. Russia was the subject in the "World Events" section. *Just my luck! An Asian country!* I knew Mrs. Kelly would use the Asian map with the big new tear in it.

First, of great interest to the class was the article about prehistoric fossils discovered in our own South Dakota Badlands. One of the nation's best-known paleontologists, Dr. James D. Bump of the South Dakota School of Mines and Technology in Rapid City, made the Badlands sound like a gold mine. He knew of no other place outside the Badlands where so many types of past life could be found. Among the fossil animal forms found that surprised us were the saber-toothed tiger, the three-toed horse, and ancestors of the camel, hog, and rhinoceros. Dr. Bump said that as many as eighteen groups of scientists were exploring the area at the same time. They were anticipating some big finds someday.

I didn't participate much because I didn't feel like it. But when the discussion continued for quite a while and I saw the clock hands move closer to recess time, I thought of some questions to ask in case I needed to drag the time out.

When the clock's hands moved to 2:15, Mrs. Kelly said, "You'll have to read the article on Russia yourselves some other time."

I felt relieved, lucky. I had been spared the embarrassment of my awful deed and the likelihood of Mrs. Kelly's anger for one day.

24

Friday at school was tense for me, as I worried about whether Mrs. Kelly would discover the ripped map. She didn't.

The only thing I wished on Saturday was for it to be over.

Finally, Sunday, the day of Matthew's baptism, was here.

I was happy that Matthew was healthy. He looked cute in his little blue knit two-piece baby suit. Mom was tying the laces of his tiny white baby shoes when I went to check on them.

"Everyone's in the car, Mom," I said.

"I guess Dad doesn't feel like honking the horn to get my ire up," she said.

That was something he did on many a Sunday morning, before Matthew was born, to tease Mom. It riled Mom a little, and Dad would chuckle when she came rushing to the car. But Dad was quiet this morning, not in a teasing mood.

"Why doesn't Matthew have a white christening gown?" I asked.

"People aren't using those as much in our church these days," she answered. "Instead, they dress their babies in very nice outfits for their baptisms. Like Matthew is wearing."

Mom looked nice in her navy suit and matching high heels. She put on her wide-brimmed red hat, secured it to her dark hair with a long hatpin she wove in and out of the back of the hat, and checked her image in the mirror.

"Time to go, Matthew!" she said, and wrapped his light blue woven blanket around him. He smiled at her when she picked him up and baby-cooed his reply.

I closed the door to the house behind her. Kim got out of the back door of the car and made me sit between Carol and her, where the hump was. Susie was in the middle in the front. Mom slid into her seat with Matthew in one arm and closed her door with the other.

It was a quiet eight-mile ride to church in town. We were the second car to park diagonally by the sidewalk that led to the little white frame church with CONCORDIA LUTHERAN CHURCH written in black letters above its double door. We were always early, and we always parked about four cars from the door, leaving the first few spots for others. This morning, as on other Sundays, we waited in the car until more people arrived.

It was a cool morning with an even blue sky above white floating clouds that looked like the pieces of cotton torn from the roll Mom used to put baby oil on Matthew's skin.

"Kim, roll your window down. I need some fresh air," I said.

"No. It's too cold," she said. "You forgot to say please, anyway."

"Well, Kid, shall we go in?" Dad asked. "Sounds like the girls are getting restless."

"Might as well," Mom said.

By now a few more cars lined the sidewalk. "Good morning" was exchanged among the adult members. Not many families with kids were there yet. They would come later.

We climbed the wooden stairs and entered the church vestibule through its open double door. We then opened the inside door and filed into the church—Carol, Kim, me, Susie, Mom with Matthew, and then Dad. Carol led us straight ahead into the third pew from the back on the right side, where we always sat.

The Hanlons, Matthew's sponsors, exchanged greetings with Mom and Dad when they came in, and sat in the pew behind us. Then the Reverend Meyer entered, carrying his black robe over his arm. He nodded brief greetings to members on his way to the little room to the left of the altar with a curtain for a door.

The light gray walls, three arched windows with colored rectangular glass on each side, and the large arched window at the back made the church light and airy. The aisle went up the middle of the church, with eight pews on the right side and five on the left starting in front of the door. There were two steps up to a platform where a small white altar, containing a shiny gold cross with Jesus hanging on it, stood against the wall. The morning sun cast warm colors through the windows on the right side.

The usher came through the door carrying a Mason jar of water and a white cloth. He walked up the aisle to the baptismal font on the left, poured the water into the basin dish, and laid the cloth on the edge.

That's for Matthew! I thought. A flutter of anticipation swept over me. I looked at Matthew, sleeping in Mom's arms.

The usher ducked behind the curtain where Reverend Meyer prepared for the service. The usher came out with a match in his hand, lifted his foot, and struck the match on his shoe before lighting a lone candle on each side of the cross. He blew out the match and walked down the aisle and out the door. I knew he would put the match in the ashtray stand just outside the door, because I'd seen him do it before. Then he'd pull the big rope to ring the bell that was in the square part of the steeple.

The service was long, especially before the baptism. Four hymns were posted in black numbers on the wooden marquee above the wall where Mrs. Johannes pumped hymn music from the organ. We sang one of the hymns at the beginning of the service. Then we confessed our sins, sang a lot of liturgy songs, and listened to Bible readings. We sang another hymn before the sermon, which I tried to listen to but fidgeted through almost as much as Susie did.

When is Reverend Meyer going to say "amen"? I wondered.

Finally, he did. Then we sang another hymn before the offering plate was passed around the pews and taken by the usher to Reverend Meyer, who placed the plate on the altar.

Reverend Meyer read a long prayer from his book—two pages long. I heard him turn the page. We prayed for the Church Universal, the government, our enemies, those who are sick and suffering. We prayed for mercy, for a prosperous harvest, for lawful occupations on land and sea, for pure arts and useful knowledge. Near the end, we thanked God for salvation. Finally I heard, ". . . world without end. Amen."

A shiver of joy ran through me. It was time for Matthew's baptism!

Reverend Meyer turned to the congregation and said, "Would the sponsors bring the infant child forward?" Mrs. Hanlon leaned over the pew and Mom reached Matthew up to her. He squirmed a little. I wondered if he would cry when he felt the water. That's usually when babies cry during their baptisms.

Mr. and Mrs. Hanlon walked to the front and stood beside the baptismal font. Reverend Meyer nodded to them and began: "Dearly Beloved." I listened intently. "We learn from the Word of God that all men from the fall of Adam are conceived and born in sin, and so are under the wrath of God, and would be lost forever unless delivered by our Lord Jesus Christ."

I'd heard those words before, but this time they sounded very serious.

"Matthew Johnson, then, is also by nature sinful and under the wrath of God."

It doesn't seem fair. He hasn't done anything wrong yet, I thought.

"But the Father of all mercy and grace hath promised and sent His Son Jesus Christ, who hath borne the sins of the whole world, and redeemed and saved little children, no less than others, from sin, death, and everlasting condemnation. He also commanded that little children should be brought to Him, and he graciously received and blessed them.

"Wherefore, I beseech you"—Reverend Meyer looked at Mr. and Mrs. Hanlon and then back at his book—"out of Christian love, to intercede for Matthew Johnson, to bring him to the Lord Jesus and to ask for His forgiveness, grace, and salvation of Christ's kingdom.

"Our Lord hath commanded baptism and hath promised in the last chapter of Mark: 'He that believeth and is baptized shall be saved.' It is meet and right that you should bring Matthew Johnson to be baptized in His name."

Reverend Meyer informed the Hanlons, as sponsors, that they were to keep him in their prayers and lend their help, especially if he lost his parents, so that he would be brought up in the true knowledge and fear of God, according to the teachings of the Lutheran Church.

"I now ask you to answer, in the name and the stead of Matthew Lee Johnson, the questions which I address to him." Reverend Meyer looked at the Hanlons again. Mrs. Hanlon was jiggling Matthew rhythmically, like women do to keep babies content. I had to stretch my neck to see over Susie's head, because she had stood up so she could see.

The Hanlons answered "I do" for Matthew several times. They denounced the devil for him. They believed in God the Father for him, Jesus Christ His only Son, and the Holy Ghost for him, the forgiveness of sins and life everlasting for him.

"Wilt thou be baptized into this Christian faith?"

The Hanlons answered, "I will." Then Mrs. Hanlon pulled the blanket away from Matthew's head and shoulders and held him sideways so his head was over the baptismal font.

Reverend Meyer leaned over and said, "Matthew Lee Johnson, I baptize thee in the name of the Father . . ." He cupped his hand with water and poured it over the top of Matthew's head. I waited for Matthew to cry, but he murmured only one "Aaa!"

Reverend Meyer continued, ". . . and of the Son . . ." Another handful of water. ". . . and of the Holy Ghost." Another handful of water. "Amen."

Done! It's done! Matthew is safe!

Reverend Meyer wiped Matthew's head with the cloth. Then he said, "Receive the sign of the holy cross, both upon the forehead . . ." He drew a cross with his hand above Matthew's forehead. ". . . And upon the breast . . ." He drew another cross above his breast. ". . . In token that thou has been redeemed by Christ the Crucified. Peace be with thee. Amen."

Reverend Meyer then addressed the congregation. "Let us pray the prayer our Lord has taught us." After the Lord's Prayer, the Hanlons returned to their seat and Mrs. Hanlon handed Matthew back to Mom. His eyes were open and he gave Mom his baby smile. She smiled, too, and kissed his forehead before pulling the blanket around his shoulders. Then she cradled him in her arms.

Dad looked at them, his brown eyes gentle and loving. Then he bowed his head.

He's praying for Roger Gene, I thought.

Mrs. Johannes started playing the tune for Hymn 300, a baptism hymn. We sang all five verses. I wasn't happy about that until the last two lines of the last verse:

> Write the name we now have given,
> Write it in the book of heaven.

I liked the idea of Matthew's name written in the book of heaven.

Then I wondered, *Is Roger Gene's name written there?*

Reverend Meyer said another prayer and gave the Lord's blessing, but my mind had wandered. I was glad the final hymn was a short one.

I shared a hymnal with Susie and was not prepared when, near the end of the hymn, she suddenly let go. The book dropped from my hand and I was embarrassed by the loud noise. I gave Susie a disgusted look when I stooped to pick it up, and then felt bad because we were in church and it was Matthew's baptism.

"I didn't mean to," she mouthed to me.

I barely paid attention to her, for when I picked up the hymnal by its open back cover, I was stunned by what I saw on the very last page of the book. At the top of the half page of text was printed:

A Short Form for Holy Baptism in Cases of Necessity.

Then in smaller print it said,

> *In urgent cases, in the absence of the Pastor, any Christian may administer Holy Baptism.*
>
> *Take water, call the child by name, pour or sprinkle the water on the head of the child, saying:*
>
> **I baptize thee in the name of the Father and of the Son and of the Holy Ghost. Amen.**
>
> *If there is time, the baptism may be preceded by the following prayer and the Lord's Prayer.*

Copies of the prayers were printed in two paragraphs. Everything fit on less than half the page. The rest of the page was blank.

When the organist played the last hymn's tune as a postlude, I was vaguely aware that Reverend Meyer came out of his little room at the front with his robe over his arm, walked down the aisle, and stopped at the edge of our pew. "Congratulations, Tony!" he said, shaking Dad's hand. "Congratulations, Leona!" he said, smiling at Mom. "I'm sorry my wife and I will not be able to join you for dinner today. We'll take a rain check. Here's Matthew's baptismal certificate, Tony." He handed Dad a white envelope and then took his place by the door to shake hands with parishioners before leaving for his other church in the country.

Several men came to shake Dad's hand and congratulate him and Mom. The women wanted peeks at Matthew. Mom put him on her shoulder so they could see him. His head was still a little wobbly but getting stronger. Mom held her hand close to his head out of habit. The women said, "He's a darling baby!" and "You look good, Leona!"

The words, the movements were all background to what I was thinking.

If only Mom and Dad had known . . .

"You have a fine baby brother, Rachel." It was the soft, kind voice of Mrs. Hammond, my Sunday school teacher, smiling at me with her violet blue eyes. I smiled back, nodding my head in agreement. Before I left the pew for class, I checked the last hymnal page again, then closed the book and placed it in the rack on the back of the pew.

The church had few people left inside—a few kids and two Sunday school teachers. Mom, Carol, and

Susie were walking out. Carol was confirmed, and since there were no classes for high school kids, she taught the youngest children in the basement, where Susie's class was also held. Kim was with her class on the left side of the church.

I followed Mrs. Hammond to the third pew on the right. Melissa and Barbara, a sixth grader, were waiting for us.

"How are you girls this morning?" Mrs. Hammond asked them.

"Fine," they answered together.

Mrs. Hammond said a short opening prayer before we opened our lesson books. The lesson topic was forgiveness. The story told of a sinful woman in St. Luke, Chapter 7. She heard that Jesus was at a Pharisee's house nearby. She went to that house and made a big fuss over Jesus. She washed his feet with her tears and then wiped them with her long hair. The Pharisee didn't think Jesus should let her touch him because she was sinful. But Jesus pointed out that she loved him very much, more than the Pharisee did. The Bible said that Jesus said to the woman, "Thy sins are forgiven" and "Thy faith hath saved thee; go in peace."

That seemed easy. Didn't she *have to be baptized?*

We took turns practicing and reciting our memory verse from Ephesians 2:8–9. "For by grace are ye saved through faith; and that not of yourselves: it is the gift of God: not of works, lest any man should boast."

It doesn't say anything about baptism.

"Mrs. Hammond?" I said.

"Yes, Rachel?"

"It doesn't say anything about baptism in the Bible verse. And it doesn't say that the sinful woman was baptized."

"No." She answered with a question mark in her voice. She knew I had more to ask.

"So why wouldn't a minister in Iowa bury a tiny baby who got sick and died in a snowstorm before *he* could be baptized?"

Mrs. Hammond looked at me, speechless.

"And his mother already had his christening gown?"

Melissa and Barbara listened, neither moving a muscle.

"Is this someone you know?" Mrs. Hammond asked.

I swallowed but managed to answer with only a slight quiver in my voice. "It was my parents' first baby, Roger Gene."

"Oh my!" Mrs. Hammond's voice was sorrowful.

"My dad was heartbroken. And since Matthew's birth he's been worrying about this again."

Mrs. Hammond's eyes were full of sympathy.

"Rachel, I'll talk to Reverend Meyer and see what answers he might have to your questions."

She checked her watch. "I see our time is up. Let's close with a prayer." She read the prayer from her teacher's manual and added her own words at the end. "Grant that there will be some answers to Rachel's questions that will give her family peace and understanding. Amen."

"Mrs. Hammond, before we go, can I show you something I saw in the hymnal?"

"Sure, Rachel."

I took a book from the rack and showed her the last page. "Is this really true? Can anyone baptize a baby in an emergency?"

"Why, yes, if they are of the Christian faith."

If only Mom and Dad had known. But how could I tell them now?

25

All day at school Monday, I feared that Mrs. Kelly would discover the big rip in the map. I was a grateful student when I boarded the bus after school, wondering how long my luck would last.

When we stepped off the bus at home, Blackie was waiting for us. Susie and I stopped to pet him. "Too bad Blackie can't go to school," Susie said.

"Blackie's a smart dog already," I said, as much to reward Blackie as to reply to Susie.

"But he doesn't have anybody to play with."

"He has us."

"But he doesn't have other dogs."

I didn't reply, because a car had turned at the mile corner. "I wonder whose car that is."

Susie went to the garage and stood on her tiptoes to look in the windows. "It's not Dad. Our car is here. The pickup, too.

"We'd better tell Mom." I turned and Susie

followed me into the house. "Car's coming, Mom!" I reported.

Mom looked out the window and saw the car driving around the bend. She quickly tidied the kitchen counter. "Girls, straighten the boots in the breezeway."

"The boots were all straightened when we came in, Mom," I said.

"Check the entry by the front door. Quick!"

I went. "Well, hi, Matthew!" I said when I saw him on his tummy on a blanket on the living room rug.

"Clean as a whistle out here!" I called loud enough so my voice would carry to the kitchen. Since Susie had started school, there weren't any of her playthings out there anymore. It was a warm sunny spot in cool weather because the walls were made of glass blocks, and Susie had often played there.

I leaned down to Matthew, who was lifting his head to try to look at me. "Someone's coming, Matthew! Maybe you'll get to see who it is, too."

"Did you see your dad anywhere outside?" Mom asked.

"Didn't see him, but the tractor garage door was open," I said.

We heard the crunch of gravel under slow-moving tires and knew the car was in our lane. Soon we saw it through the kitchen window.

"Why, it's Reverend Meyer!" Mom exclaimed.

"He's coming to the front door. Rachel, let him in, will you? I'll be right there. I have to dry my hands and take off my apron."

The doorbell rang just as I got to the door. Susie came, too. I opened the door.

"Hello, Rachel! Susie!" Reverend Meyer said.

"Hello, Reverend Meyer. Come in!" I said. "Mom will be here in a minute."

"I see I timed this right. I was hoping you children would be home from school." Reverend Meyer stepped inside.

Carol and Kim had heard the doorbell and emerged from their room to see who it was.

"Hello, Carol! Kim!" Reverend Meyer said.

"Hello, Reverend Meyer!" they replied.

"Reverend! Welcome!" Mom greeted him as she entered the living room.

"Sorry I couldn't call, Leona."

"It's pretty hard to call someone without a phone," Mom replied, smiling.

Carol, Kim, and I remembered our manners and resisted the urge to look at each other and roll our eyes as if to say, *Tell us about it.*

"Yes, it is," Reverend Meyer said, laughing gently.

"Did you want to see Tony?" Mom asked.

"Actually, I would like to speak with your whole family, Leona. It's about baptism and some of our beliefs."

"Oh!" Mom's voice conveyed curiosity.

I was curious, too. *Has Mrs. Hammond talked with him already?* I wondered. *Was this about Roger Gene?*

"I'll send one of the kids to find Tony."

"You won't have to send anyone. Here he comes." Carol had spotted him through a kitchen window walking to the house. The door opened and soon Dad joined us. He had removed his farmer's cap, but the cap line still showed in the hair around his head.

"Hello, Tony!" Reverend Meyer said, extending his hand.

"Reverend!" Dad nodded and shook his hand.

"Have a seat, please, Reverend Meyer!" Mom gestured to the sofa. "Would you like a cup of coffee?"

"Yes, thank you, if it's not any trouble."

"No trouble at all. It's even ready.

"Tony?" Mom asked.

"Sure. Thanks!" Dad sat in his chair but did not lean back.

"As I told Leona, Tony, I'd like to address the topic of baptism with your family."

"Baptism?" Dad said. "Why sure."

"I'll wait until Leona gets back," Reverend Meyer said.

Carol picked up Matthew and sat in Mom's rocking chair. Kim and I sat on one section of the divided sofa and Susie sat on the section by Reverend Meyer.

"Do you like school?" he asked Susie.

"I love school," Susie answered. "I can read already!"

"Reading is a wonderful gift," said Reverend Meyer.

Mom brought the coffee in her good china cups and saucers with the thin border of flowers around the edge. She sat on a chair near the kitchen door.

Reverend Meyer sipped his coffee. "Good coffee, Leona!"

"Thank you."

"I'm here because Mrs. Hammond called me with some questions that Rachel had regarding baptism." He nodded at me. "Do I understand that your first child was a son who died in infancy before he could be baptized?"

Dad was silent.

"Yes. Roger Gene," Mom said. "He died of the flu when he was a month old."

Susie's eyes widened in surprise.

"This is the first that Susie knows of this," Mom added, smiling apologetically at her.

"Of course," Reverend Meyer said. He smiled at Susie sympathetically.

"He died before we had a chance to baptize him," Dad added sadly. "We had every intention. Leona had his christening gown, but that winter of 1937 was bad, the worst in memory, and we couldn't get to church. Then our baby got ill suddenly . . . ," Dad said, his voice fading, ". . . and he died."

"I'm very sorry," Reverend Meyer said, and waited a few seconds before continuing.

"Is it true that the minister of your church denied your baby a Christian burial?"

"Yes," Mom and Dad answered together.

"Were you members in good standing, with regular church attendance?"

"Yep!" Dad answered. "As much as the weather allowed."

"And it was a Lutheran church?"

"Oh yes!" Mom answered. "Tony wouldn't be anything but a Lutheran!"

"Well, unfortunately, in my view, we have considerable disagreement within the Lutheran clergy concerning Holy Baptism—and other matters as well. There is a segment of clergy who adhere strictly to the interpretation that baptism is necessary to enter the Kingdom of God. No exceptions. I fear that the differences in interpretation are such that we will eventually be two separate Lutheran church bodies."

Matthew squirmed and made baby groans. All eyes moved from Reverend Meyer to him. Carol smiled an apology, placed him on her shoulder, patted his back, and he was content again.

Reverend Meyer smiled, took another sip of coffee, and continued. "Your former minister was one of those who adhere to that strict interpretation of baptism. And I'm truly sorry for the anguish this has caused you these many years."

Dad nodded, accepting his sympathy.

"I reread some church arguments on this issue, and they state that the same church law applies to infants who could not receive Holy Baptism as to those who were stillborn. In fact, an exact quote is: 'We may well commend such as could not be baptized to the infinite mercy of God.' The church *does* make exceptions to the baptism requirement in these cases.

"Your first-born *is,* Tony and Leona, in the loving arms of our gracious God. There is no doubt in my mind."

Dad sighed, a slow quiet release of breath.

A feeling of relief moved through the room.

Mom caught tears with her finger before they could fall.

Dad absorbed Reverend Meyer's words with quiet gratitude. There was a glint of moisture in his eyes.

Thank you, God!

"I have a proposal that I think will bring peaceful closure for you in this matter," Reverend Meyer continued. "You can have your infant son's body disinterred, transferred here, and reburied in our local cemetery. It would be a joy for me to conduct a Christian burial service for him." He paused, allowing Dad and Mom time with the idea.

Dad smiled, shaking his head. "You know, Reverend, it's funny you should suggest that, because I was thinking just last week when I was visiting our son's grave that it would be a good thing to rebury him here.

"Don't you think it's a good idea, Kid?" Dad asked Mom.

"Definitely! It was meant to be. This will be good for all of us."

"That settles it!" Dad's voice was softer, warmer, more relaxed than I'd heard for a long time.

"What's involved?" he asked Reverend Meyer.

"It's not as involved as one might think. I can make most of the arrangements by phone. There will be a fee for disinterment, opening the grave and recovering it, and there will be a fee at the cemetery here for reburial that covers the cost of digging the grave and covering it. This is arranged through a funeral director on that end, who will coordinate the opening of the grave and take care of all the paperwork. Then the funeral director here will make arrangements on this end."

"How is the body transferred?" Dad asked.

"If the casket is in good condition, you may transport the body."

"Roger Gene was buried in a steel casket," Mom said.

"Then the casket should be in excellent condition.

"I think sooner is better than later," Reverend Meyer suggested. "In fact, if I am able to contact everyone, I will arrange this coming Friday for disinterment, and then a reburial service for Saturday morning. Does that work?"

"Friday and Saturday will work fine!" Dad said.

"Do you have a family plot here?" Reverend Meyer asked.

"No, but we'll have one as soon as I can meet with the cemetery supervisor," Dad said. "If you like, why don't you come here Friday morning and I'll drive to Iowa. I'll have the trunk ready to transport the casket."

"Very good! I'll arrange it." And with that, Reverend Meyer rose.

"And now," he began in his praying voice, which prompted us all to bow our heads, "may the grace of our Lord Jesus Christ and the love of God and the communion of the Holy Ghost be with you all. Amen."

"Thank you, Reverend!" Dad said, rising to shake hands. His voice sounded like his heart was so full of gratitude that it would burst if any more got in.

"Goodbye, girls!" Reverend Meyer nodded to us.

Mom and Dad walked with him to the door. "You are a blessing in our lives, Reverend!" Mom said.

"That's a heartwarming thank-you, Leona.

“What time would you like to leave Friday morning, Tony?”

“It’s a good five-hour drive. How about seven? We should be able to be home by eight that night.”

“I’ll be here at seven.”

The whole family stood in the front entry. Silent, grateful, we watched Reverend Meyer get into his car and drive away.

26

The anticipation of bringing Roger Gene home to be buried sparked an energy in our family that matched the electricity of the crisp October air. Frost had whitened the grass every morning that week.

Dad was a different person. I heard him whistling and singing on the tractor while out plowing late Tuesday afternoon. The chilly dense air of autumn carried his singing across the fields. Dad yodeled and sang nonsense syllables that sounded like warm-up drills. He had a pleasant singing voice, but he would have been mortified if he knew anyone could hear him.

Mom was happy, too. She didn't have to worry about Dad being sad. Now that Matthew wasn't a newborn anymore, she would be able to go with Dad on some of the nearby cattle-buying trips. She went with Dad on Tuesday to choose a family plot in the cemetery on the other edge of town, a half-mile from the schoolyard.

Matthew was growing stronger and could roll over by himself. He loved attention, rewarding everyone with smiles and baby gurgles.

Susie, Carol, Kim, and I enjoyed school.

But Wednesday turned out to be an unlucky day for me.

Mrs. Kelly gave us another multiplication facts test. I panicked when she announced that it was not the usual one in our arithmetic book. Instead, she held the tests in her hands. She was giving it to the fifth and sixth grades at the same time.

She held up a test to show that the whole page was covered with facts, in purplish ink. "There are one hundred facts on this sheet of paper," she said. She smiled that devilish, challenging smile. "Before the year is up, every fifth grader should strive to finish in four minutes, every sixth grader in three minutes."

A low groan rumbled across the room. Mrs. Kelly chuckled and then encouraged us. "Many of you may be able to do that today. If not, you do have most of the school year to work at it.

"I'll place the test face-down on your desk. Leave the paper face-down. Write your name and date at the top left on the back and don't turn it over until I say 'begin.'"

When she laid my paper down, she flashed her devilish grin at me. I felt a pinch of guilt about my method of memorizing the answers. I flushed, too, remembering the rip in the map, and thanked my lucky stars that she hadn't pulled the map down since then.

"When you are finished, turn the paper upside down and write your time below the date," directed Mrs. Kelly. "Once your paper is turned over, you can't look at it again. Today, you will be given five minutes. Are there any questions?"

No one raised a hand.

"Then begin!" A flutter filled the room when everyone flipped the papers over to begin.

The whole page of facts was intimidating. But once I started and finished a couple of rows, it seemed possible.

After a few minutes, gasps of relief were heard on the sixth-grade side as kids finished. I still had two rows to go. I glanced at the board to check the time. Mrs. Kelly had written "2:50."

I heard someone on our side turn his paper. Probably Darren. Melissa turned hers when I had two more to go.

My time was 3:30. Several sixth graders were done and waiting. More fifth graders were finishing. Only a few were still writing when Mrs. Kelly called, "Time!"

Melissa and I exchanged papers. I had five wrong. Melissa, only one. Darren, two.

After that test, I decided I would just practice the facts for faster recall rather than memorize the answers. *Besides, who knows how many times Mrs. Kelly will change the test?*

During the last hour of the day, a knock on the classroom door interrupted our history lesson just as Rita, a sixth grader, asked an interesting question. Sixth graders were allowed to participate in fifth-grade history because our books were new and they didn't have this lesson last year.

"Excuse me a minute, Rita," Mrs. Kelly said. She opened the door and was handed a stack of large envelopes, which we recognized as our school picture packets. Looks of anticipation and anxiety were exchanged around the room.

My feeling was dread.

Mrs. Kelly placed the packets on her desk, smiled that knowing smile, and continued with the lesson. "Now, Rita, please repeat your question," she said.

"How can they say that Hernando de Soto *discovered* the Mississippi River when Indians were already there?"

"Hmmm. You've asked a very good question. How would *you* rewrite the statement, Rita?" Mrs. Kelly asked her.

"Well . . . they could write that Hernando de Soto

was the first *white* man to *explore* the Mississippi River."

"Very good! Very good, Rita! That statement would reflect the event more accurately."

She looked around the room to give others a chance to comment. No one did. I think most of us were anxious to get those picture packets and didn't want to prolong the lesson with questions.

"Well, so much for history today," Mrs. Kelly said, laughing, and put her book with others between the black metal bookends on her desk.

"Now, pictures!" She scanned a sheet of paper that was on top of the stack, then informed us. "The price lists are inside the envelopes, so make sure you get those home to your parents. You do not have to purchase any pictures. Or you may purchase all of them. Or some of them. The whole package is one dollar and fifty cents. Class pictures are separate for fifty cents each. I'll post one of those near the door for you to look at when you leave."

Mrs. Kelly started handing out the packets, saying the names aloud. I took my three-ring notebook from my desk so I could slip the packet between its covers. The large black-and-white portrait of the person was looking out from a window cut into the envelope. I didn't want anyone to see what I feared was looking out of my window.

"Melissa." Mrs. Kelly handed Melissa her packet. Melissa seemed embarrassed and she giggled, holding her packet against her so no one could see. I sent her a questioning glance. Her picture had to be perfect. She turned it sideways so I could see. It *was* perfect. Her hair was beautiful, with a sheen on top from the light. Her smile showed nice teeth. Her blue eyes with long lashes sparkled even in black and white. I nodded my head in hearty approval. She smiled her thanks.

Winnie tapped her shoulder from behind, a "let-me-see" tap. Melissa held the packet up. Ellen, who had moved up behind me after Rebecca left, leaned forward to see, too. Winnie and Ellen also gave her hearty approval nods. She laid the packet on her desktop.

"Rachel." It was my turn. Mrs. Kelly handed my packet to me. I saw what I feared and instantly slipped it inside the notebook.

When Melissa, Winnie, and Ellen indicated they wanted to see, I shook my head. "Come on," whispered Ellen, tapping me on the shoulder.

I shook my head and looked at them, pleading with my eyes, *Please don't ask me.*

Winnie shrugged her shoulders and they let it drop.

When Mrs. Kelly handed out the last packet, she announced, "The school would like your picture money paid by next Friday. If you don't keep them, the packets are to be returned by then also. Any questions?"

"Do we pay for the class pictures by Friday, too?" Lance asked.

"Yes. All picture money is due next Friday. Any other questions?" She paused. "If not, then it's time to get ready for dismissal."

After dismissal, we crowded around the door to see the class picture. I was satisfied with my picture there.

A lot of kids showed their pictures to each other, even on the bus. I didn't.

Susie showed hers. Her picture was very cute. Her long dark eyelashes outlining her brown eyes really showed up in the large window picture. She smiled and there were no spaces between her teeth.

When we got off the bus, there was a note in Mom's handwriting on the back of an old business letter on the kitchen table.

Went to Aberdeen for some things.
Should be home by 5.
Feed the cattle.
Mom & Dad

I had about half an hour to feel sorry for myself about my pictures. Carol, Kim, and Susie were showing theirs to each other. I refused. Instead I went to my room, locked the door so Susie wouldn't come in, and looked at the portrait in the packet window. There were the stubborn bangs. But worse, there were my front teeth with the spaces.

27

At about five o'clock, Susie and I started glancing out the windows for signs of Mom and Dad. Carol and Kim were still feeding the cattle. A few minutes later, we saw our maroon Pontiac on the mile road, creating a dusty plume behind it. We went out to wait for them. Blackie came around from the side of the garage to see what was going on.

"Here they come, Blackie!" I scratched the top of his head. "I bet they ordered a tombstone for Roger Gene."

When Mom got out of the car, she had Matthew in her arms and gripped a shopping sack in her fingers. "Grab the sack for me, please, Rachel!"

"What's in here?"

"A piece of red satin."

"Red satin?"

"Yes. We're going to spread that over the floor of our trunk under Roger Gene's casket."

"Did you get a tombstone for Roger Gene?"

"A very nice one. It'll be in place by Saturday morning."

Dad got out of the car and opened the trunk. He seemed relaxed and purposeful. "When you get a chance, Kid, I could use some old rags."

"I'll send Rachel out with some in a minute," Mom said. I followed her into the house and set her sack on the table.

I was curious about what was in the trunk. "I know where the rags are, Mom. I'll get them."

"Get a couple old frayed hand towels. Those will work better than old diapers or dishtowels."

When I brought the rags to Dad, I saw that the trunk was amazingly clean. A new can of kerosene and a can of pearl lacquer were in a sack. Everything else had been taken out of the trunk except the spare tire and the tire jack, which were pushed to the far back. And the trunk had been vacuumed.

"I also need the soft metal brush and the medium paintbrush," Dad said. "They're hanging on nails in this garage. See if you can find them for me."

I remembered seeing them and found them right away.

"What's all this stuff for?" I asked.

"Roger Gene's casket. It'll be all rusty after seventeen years." He was matter-of-fact. "I'll wire-brush the rust off, clean the steel good with kerosene, and paint this pretty pearl lacquer on it before we rebury him." He nodded, determined. "Roger Gene will have a new burial with a proper service."

It was good to hear enthusiasm and cheer in Dad's voice.

"Can . . . may I go along to Iowa?"

"No." But he was sorry about saying no and explained. "Not even your mother is going. We decided it would be best that just Reverend Meyer and I go. There shouldn't be any complications, but just in case, it's better that just the two of us go."

Later that evening Mom was in the kitchen ironing the bright red satin cloth. I showed her my pictures. "They're awful! The photographer made me laugh and then he took my picture. I look awful! I'm not going to keep them!"

"Nonsense, Rachel! You're too sensitive about your teeth. You are a lovely girl with a sweetness to match. You keep your pictures. You'll change your mind."

"No I won't!"

"Your dad has already written the check for everyone's pictures and given it to Carol to take to the superintendent's office tomorrow." She moved the cloth to a section that hadn't been ironed.

"Oh, all right," I said. *I'll keep them because they're paid for. But no one at school will see them,* I thought.

"Help me roll this satin, Rachel. I don't want any wrinkles in it." Mom put the satin between two large terry towels and we carefully rolled it like a strawberry jellyroll before it's cut into pieces.

"Rachel! Here's a ping pong of me!" Susie handed a little school picture of herself to me when I came into our room.

Why can't I be this cute?

"Look on the back!" Susie said.

I turned it over and saw "To Rachel from Susie" written in beginner's printing.

"Can I have one of you?"

"No."

"Why not?"

"I haven't cut them up yet."

"When you cut them up, will you give me one?"

"No."

"Pleeease?"

"Only if you *promise* not to take it to school."

"Why not?"

"Because!"

"Okay."

"Cross your heart and hope to die?"

"Cross my heart and hope to die." She drew an X across her chest.

I didn't cut up my ping pongs that night. And I didn't bring any pictures to school the next day.

"Trade pictures, Rachel?" several kids asked.

"I'm not trading. My pictures are awful!"

My best friends gave me pictures of themselves anyway. Even Lance gave me one.

Mrs. Kelly handed the classroom pictures to us just before dismissal. She had received a list earlier, after a knock on the door, of families that had paid in the superintendent's office.

I liked the picture. Everyone looked good. I'm glad I was sitting, because that raised my jeans legs enough to see the tops of my boots. The group picture would be my memento of this year's class.

Before I walked out the door, I saw the stack of achievement tests in Mrs. Kelly's cupboard behind her desk when she opened the door. She probably had them all checked and the results would be known in November during parent-teacher conferences.

If only we could have taken the tests this week or next week. Dad's happier now that Roger Gene's getting a proper service. And I'd probably do a lot better.

When we got home from school, Dad was cleaning the car. I saw the wet spot with a few soap bubbles on the gravel where he had emptied the pail of dirty water. He was wiping the car with a yellowish tan suede cloth.

"Is that a *chamois?*"

"Yep!"

"What's it feel like?" He handed it to me. "It's soft!" I handed it back.

"It wipes the car and doesn't leave any spots. This car looks about as good as it can."

The inside was spotless, too.

Blackie was circling around the car, his tail wagging. He sensed the excitement.

Dad would leave early tomorrow, perhaps before any of us girls were up.

When he returned from Iowa tomorrow night, this car would contain the casket and body of his first baby son, my brother.

28

Mom was sipping coffee and Dad was finishing a bowl of oatmeal when I walked sleepily into the kitchen the next morning. The sky was dark, with a pale pink slowly painting itself above the east horizon.

Dad was dressed in good work clothes, a western shirt, navy denim jeans, and his in-between pair of cowboy boots.

Carol and Kim came out of their room too, followed shortly by a sleepy Susie. Only Matthew was sleeping.

"Do we have to feed the cattle?" Carol asked.

"It's done," Dad said.

"Here comes Reverend Meyer!" Mom said. We looked out the window and watched the moving light separate into headlights as it drew closer.

"This is a big day, Kid!" Dad rose from the table.

"It's a wonderful day!" Mom kissed Dad at the kitchen door. "I'll be thinking about you."

"I want to kiss you too, Daddy!"

"Okay, Susie." She hurried to the door and Dad leaned down for her kiss on his cheek.

"Greet Reverend Meyer and have a safe trip," Mom said before Dad left through the breezeway door.

We could see little in the dark, but we watched and waved through the kitchen and then the living room windows as Dad and Reverend Meyer drove away in our shiny Pontiac.

—

It was hard for me to concentrate at school. I imagined where Dad and Reverend Meyer were, what they might be doing. Just before "Literature Aloud," I visualized them lifting a rusty casket from a small, open grave. But while Mrs. Kelly read, I sat riveted, waiting to hear if Mafatu would survive the sea journey home in his hand-carved sailing canoe, which held tips of the octopus arms he had cut off with his knife, his necklace of boar's teeth, and his splendid hand-wrought spear. All this after escaping the eaters-of-men who had chased him far out to sea.

Sighs escaped all around the room when Mrs. Kelly smiled and closed the book after reading the proclamation of Mafatu's father to his people: "Here is my son come home from the sea. Mafatu, Stout Heart. A brave name for a brave boy!"

—

That night, while Susie and I watched out the window, we listened to *The Lone Ranger* and then *Mr. Keen, Tracer of Lost Persons* on the radio.

"It's only seven, girls," Mom said. "Even if everything goes as planned, they won't be here before eight."

"I can stay up till they come, can't I, Mom?"

"Yes, Susie. This is a very special occasion."

Mom was in her rocking chair feeding Matthew his bedtime bottle. His eyes were still open.

"Matthew will probably be sleeping when Dad gets home, huh, Mom?" Susie asked.

"Probably."

"No he won't!" I exclaimed. "Here they come!" A light was at the mile corner.

"There's a light? You're not kidding?" Mom asked.

"There's a light! Here they come! Here they come!" Susie danced around.

"Don't get your hopes up too high. It could be someone else," Mom said.

Hearing the commotion, Carol came to look out the window, waving her hand to dry fresh fingernail polish. Kim came, too, her hair already pinned up for the night.

"The car's coming around the bend," I reported. "It's crossing the bridge. Turning the corner. Driving up the little hill." Then it was turning into our lane, which everyone could see through the big picture window.

"That's our car!"

The four of us rushed to the kitchen window facing the garage driveway. Reverend Meyer got out, and in the headlights, we saw him open the garage door so Dad could drive in. We had the garage light on and the breezeway door to the garage open before the car was parked and the double garage door rolled to a stop above it.

Reverend Meyer greeted us with a warm smile. "Hello, girls!" he said.

Dad got out and went to the rear of the car. "Would you like a bite to eat and some coffee before you leave, Reverend?"

"Thanks, Tony, but no. Mrs. Meyer will be anxious for me to get home, too, so I'll be on my way."

They shook hands, firmly, respectfully.

We waited in the doorway.

"We'll see you tomorrow, at eleven," Dad said.

"A blessed night to you." The reverend waved to us, including us in his blessing.

We watched him drive away, silent, the weight of the moment sinking in.

Dad was solemn. “Is your mother coming out?”

“I’ll check.” I ran to the living room. Mom, holding Matthew against her shoulder, was slowly rocking him. Her free hand wiped tears from her eyes. I paused briefly. “Mom, Dad wonders if you’re coming out.”

“I’ll be right there.”

“I’ll tell him.” I hurried back to the garage. “She’ll be right here,” I reported.

Carol, Kim, and Susie had moved to the rear of the car, waiting with Dad. Beyond the open garage door, a blue-black sky covered our farm and fields. A patch of paler sky hinted where the sun had disappeared. In the east, a full moon cast its early glow. Ours was the only human light visible.

Footsteps announced Mom’s coming. She held Matthew in her arms, facing out. “Hello, Kid. I’m glad your trip went well.”

“Remarkably well.”

Mom joined us at the rear of the car.

“Is everyone ready?” Dad’s eyes surveyed us. I wondered if anyone else’s heart was pounding like mine.

Susie pressed close to me, sought my hand. We locked fingers.

Dad turned the key in the trunk's lock and lifted the lid. There, gleaming in the middle of red satin, was a small, fine pearl-white casket. On the top was the raised figure of a lamb by a cross in an oval of leaves and flowers.

"Don't touch the casket," Dad warned softly. "I don't think it's dry." That explained the edges of white cloth outlining the bottom of the casket, protecting the satin. "We'll leave the trunk lid up and it should be dry by morning."

"You did a wonderful job, Kid. It's beautiful," Mom said.

Dad nodded, thanking her with a warm smile.

We stood together in a semicircle by the open trunk. Carol, Kim, me, Susie—in age order. Dad and Mom, with Matthew, like protective ends. We stood, silent, not wanting to interrupt the sense of connection.

—

I lay awake late that night, listening to Dad's gentle voice telling the details of the day to Mom.

Their muted conversation in the kitchen was the first thing I heard Saturday morning.

Quiet anticipation marked our chores and a simple cereal breakfast. Mom prepared food for the noon dinner she was serving with the Reverend and Mrs.

Meyer as guests after Roger Gene's burial. Midmorning, we dressed in our church clothes, the ones we wore for Matthew's baptism.

Dad looked nice in his brown suit, his eyes happy. He had tested the lacquer and said it was dry. After we were ready and assembled, Dad touched his index finger under the rim of the casket to make sure. He nodded and removed the white cloth under it before closing the trunk.

Blackie was pacing excitedly around us. I was sorry he couldn't go. It seemed like he should be part of this.

We left early, drove slow the eight miles, stirring little dust on the gravel roads. The drying cornfields along the sides of the roads reminded me of crowds along a parade route.

We were the first ones to arrive. At the edge of the cemetery, a fresh mound of dirt marked a new grave. Dad drove to it. A small deep rectangle had been dug into the brown earth. Dry weather and frost had turned the grass brown. At the head of the grave was a tombstone of shiny black granite, except where the carving was lighter, grayish. On the upper part, a cross with a wreath of flowers was carved inside an oval. One side of the oval was an angel figure facing in. On the lower part was carved an inscription:

ROGER GENE JOHNSON
CHILD OF GOD
INFANT SON OF A.& L. JOHNSON
DEC. 17, 1936–FEB. 6, 1937
BURIED HERE 1954

Soon, the Reverend and Mrs. Meyer and the funeral director arrived. Following greetings and handshakes, Dad opened the trunk and he and the funeral director carried the casket to the grassy side of the grave. Reverend Meyer beckoned us to gather round the casket.

In the cool cloudless morning, with the sun warming our backs, Reverend Meyer's voice spoke kindness. His words were comforting, assuring, loving, convincing. From his first words, "Dearly beloved of God and family of Roger Gene Johnson . . . ," to ". . . Peace be with you. Amen!" When he finished, we knew, we *all* knew—somehow, I think Matthew knew, too—that Roger Gene's soul was safe in heaven.

Epilogue

After Roger Gene's new burial, life returned to normal in our house. We never forgot Reverend Meyer's goodness. I was glad that he included information about emergency baptism in a sermon a few weeks later. I hadn't told Mom and Dad about the last page in the hymnal because I didn't want to be the one to make them feel bad that they hadn't known—that Dad hadn't needed to be worried all those years.

School was great. I did better than I thought on the achievement tests. Came in second in the class. Darren was first again.

When Mrs. Kelly finally pulled down the Asian map, to my surprise, she didn't blink an eye and didn't say a word. I never did figure out why. The rip was still there, big as I remembered. I was never brave enough to confess. I couldn't stand the thought of Mrs. Kelly thinking ill of me.

Afterword

Although fictionalized for this story, my parents Anton and Leona Meier were faced with the sudden death of their infant son, Roger Gene, during the horrendous winter of 1937 in northwest Iowa. When the minister of their church refused to give their son a Christian burial, they appealed to the Reverend Clarence G. Meyer, who did, and who assured and comforted them in this matter. They were, and I am—though this event was only recently revealed to me—forever grateful to the late Reverend Meyer. My parents eventually had four daughters, one son, and another younger daughter. I am the third daughter.

Acknowledgments

I'd like to thank the Reverend Dr. Kenneth Heinitz, of Oak Park, Illinois, for his information regarding baptismal practices in the Lutheran Church, and funeral director James Furlong, of Galena, Illinois, for information on disinterment and reburial.

A Final Note

As this novel neared completion, the community of the little prairie town of Cresbard decided they could no longer sustain their school. After ninety-three years of sheltering teachers and students engaged in education, the school, with its large wooden doors and shiny brass hardware, was closed in 2004.